Bolan's Law

Not only did the Mafia want Mack Bolan's head in a sack, but the entire police establishment, including various federal agencies, wanted him put behind bars.

It was only recently that an official move from the White House had quietly "pardoned" Bolan. Sure, he had broken practically every law in the book, many times over. But, finally, someone realized that Bolan was something different, something perhaps beyond ordinary legislation.

The motivations of this superb warrior had nothing to do with any vendetta or revenge mentality. Bolan's commitment was much too wide and far too deep to be powered by such shallow preoccupations. His family tragedy, which had sparked this long campaign, was simply an awakening to truth.

Bolan had broken the law, indeed, but not out of disrespect for the law. He had seen that there was no other way to preserve the law for those who deserved its protection.

He'd proclaim his own law, and declare war as well. It seemed to be the only way.

And it worked.

At least it had up until today. For every day was a new test and a renewed battle in Bolan's relentless war.

the EXECUTIONER #37

FRIDAY'S FEAST

by Don Pendleton

PINNACLE BOOKS   LOS ANGELES

EXECUTIONER #37: FRIDAY'S FEAST

Copyright © 1979 by Don Pendleton

An original Pinnacle Books edition, published for the first time anywhere.

First printing, November 1979

ISBN: 0-523-40337-2

Cover illustration by Gil Cohen

Printed in the United States of America

PINNACLE BOOKS, INC.
2029 Century Park East
Los Angeles, California 90067

For the survivors of 5th JASCO,
wherever you are. God keep.

The guests are met, the feast is set:
May'st hear the merry din.
—Coleridge (*The Ancient Mariner*)

This is the sorrowful story
   Told as the twilight fails
And the monkeys walk together
   Holding their neighbour's tails.
—Kipling (*The Legends of Evil*)

Welcome to the feast, brothers.
But I suggest you hold each other's tails.
—Mack Bolan

FRIDAY'S FEAST

PROLOGUE

A GMC motorhome wheeled slowly through the predawn darkness of Glen Burnie, a Baltimore suburb on the Annapolis road. It pulled into a small motel, and halted opposite the darkened office. A smallish, dapper man emerged from the shadows of the building and stepped aboard the waiting vehicle. He was met at the door by a tall man wearing denims, and the two embraced like brothers long separated. And they were brothers, of a sort. The small man was Leo Turrin, a federal undercover agent who had labored diligently for years to bring down the Mafia from within. The other was Mack Bolan, also known as the Executioner—a one-man army who had vowed to "shake their house down" (the Mafia) and very nearly had, as the result of more than thirty brilliant campaigns dedicated to that goal.

The motorhome proceeded on through the parking lot and reentered the sparse traffic flow on Highway 2, a pretty, dark-haired woman at the wheel. She was April Rose, a federal technician under White House appointment to covertly support Bolan's "second-mile effort" to finally and fully dismantle the Mafia's American apparatus. She had watched the emotional reunion via the rear-view mirror, and now held up a hand to acknowledge the restrained introduction: "April, this is Sticker."

"Sticker" was understandably shy about showing his face, even to a fellow operative who really had no need to know his true identity. He remained in the shadows amidships, tossing forward a subdued greeting to the lady.

The two men went into the war room and sat at the small plot table. Bolan poured coffee and asked his friend, "How's it swinging, pal?"

"About the same," Turrin replied casually. "Largest problem, lately, is to keep ahead of the cuts. You know. It keeps getting harder to come down on the right side."

"Fewer sides," Bolan suggested, with a grin.

"Exactly." Turrin tasted his coffee, then said, "Guess I'm about to get kicked upstairs and out of the game entirely. Just between us idiots, I'm not a damned bit sorry about that. I'm sick of the life, Sarge."

Yes. Bolan could understand that. As April Rose had recently observed, it was not a life at all, but a sort of death. Angelina Turrin would no doubt heartily agree with that reading.

"When do you make the move?" Bolan inquired.

Turrin replied, "I guess it's wired to coincide with your large leap forward. As if you didn't know." He grinned. "Hal told me the story. Some of it, anyway. And I want you to know that I said not 'yes,' but, 'Hell, yes.'"

"Hal" was Harold Brognola, the chief fed. Through him, the White House had made Mack Bolan an offer which no sane man could refuse. Even so, Bolan had found the decision very difficult. He'd accepted the president's offer—as head of a new super-secret security group—but it was a conditional acceptance. First, and Bolan had made this quite clear, he'd wanted time to mount a final offensive in his personal war against the American crime kingdoms. Secondly, he'd reserved the right to hand-pick his own force to man the new agency. His first pick had been Leo Turrin.

He told Turrin, now, "It could be from frying pan to fire, pal."

"I still say, 'Hell, yes,'" Turrin replied, grinning. He sipped his coffee and showed dancing eyes above the rim of the cup. "Hal says they're going to give you a hero's burial. In Arlington, maybe."

"No way," Bolan said. "I already have a headstone . . . in Pittsfield. That's where the bones will lie . . . where they belong." His voice went a bit cold. "That's really where I died, Leo."

The little man frowned and said, "Yeah. I know." It was difficult to talk about such things.

3

"I, uh, guess I never told you how terrible I felt about, uh, all . . . about your family and all that. Your sister was a damned sweet kid and, uh, a lot like you in many ways. What do you hear from Johnny, these days?"

Johnny was the kid brother, sole survivor of the family tragedy, which had brought Mack Bolan home from an Asian war and into war everlasting on the home front. But Johnny's name was no longer Bolan—perhaps never would be again.

The eyes brightened as Bolan told Turrin, "I hear he's doing great. Growing like a weed in that Big Sky country."

"You're keeping wires on him, eh?"

"Very loosely," Bolan explained. "I don't want to jeopardize his cover. And, uh, it's better this way. Give him a chance for a normal—"

"Bull," said Turrin.

"That the way you see it?"

"Uh-huh. The kid idolizes you, Sarge. He'll never forget. And pretty soon he'll be at the age where he can make his own decisions. You'd better be thinking about that."

"I have," Bolan admitted. "Maybe . . . after we've interred the bones of Mack Bolan once and for all . . . well, it'll be a new life. If Johnny wants . . . uh, let's just say I'll be looking through different eyes. And we'll wait and see."

Turrin was beaming. "This new life, guy. Is the leap still scheduled for Sunday?"

"If Sunday ever comes, yeah."

4

"You starting to have doubts?"

The big man chuckled drily. "The doubts started, pal, with Uncle Sergio's first cut. And they've grown geometrically."

"Know what you mean," Turrin muttered. He took a long pull at the coffee, and wiped his lips with the back of his hand. "Seems like two or three lifetimes since . . . God, it's been a long road, hasn't it? Sometimes I wake up in the middle of the night in a cold sweat wondering where it would all be right now if you'd never come home from 'Nam. You know what I mean? When I think of all the—God, the Mob had this country in its pocket. We were scrambling around trying to get them on traffic offenses or whatever. Meanwhile they were sprinkling salt and pepper on the whole country, and starting to carve it for the feast. Thought they were God, for God's sake. Damned near were. Not even the President of the United States was safe from their damned *vendettas*. *Now* look at—hey, what I said . . . about, you know, sick of the life . . . I didn't mean . . . I got no regrets about anything. I'd do it all again. With you, I mean."

Bolan was deeply touched by that. But he grinned and said, "You'd do it again without me, guy."

"Well, you know what I mean."

Yes, Bolan knew what he meant. He said, "Thanks, Leo. Same here. Just wish I had a better feel for how far we've actually come. What's the mood in New York?"

"Desperate," the little guy replied. "This past week has taken a hell of a toll." He lit two cigarettes and handed one to Bolan. "You're hitting them where it really hurts, now. Deep in the moneybags. Ever since the Tennessee thing. Every day brings a new, staggering loss. I don't know how much more they can take of that. Hey, we both know, attrition at the top hasn't bothered them all that much. You whack one of these guys and five more spring up to compete for his place in the pecking order. But when you start whacking the *money*pots . . . well, say, the favorite joke around New York these days has to do with which family is going to the welfare today. And it's not a very funny joke. I mean, like, it's a whisper joke and you're very careful who you're whispering at."

Bolan smiled thinly as he commented, "Like, you wouldn't whisper it to Marco Minotti."

"Especially not to Marco," Turrin agreed, chuckling.

"What's his status?" Bolan wondered. "As of Wednesday night?"

"Very delicate," said the undercover fed. "The New Mexico thing was going to make him boss of bosses, you know. He came home with his ass in his hands, instead, and he's been swinging slowly in the breeze ever since. As of about three hours ago, though, Marco was beginning to revive a bit."

"Because of Florida?"

"Because of Florida, yeah. When Marco ate

6

the dust of White Sands, all the gossip suddenly had Tom Santelli at the top of the order. But then before anyone could catch their breath, you had Santelli on the ropes in Florida and another gold mine was . . . well, they were still trying to calculate the losses when I left there three hours ago."

"So the mood is grim."

"The mood is damned grim, yeah," Turrin said. "That's why I'm here. I'm carrying a message to Santelli."

"What's the message?"

"Do or die."

"Do what?"

"Stop Mack Bolan in Baltimore."

Bolan took a long pull at the cigarette, and blew thoughtful patterns of smoke toward the ceiling of the warwagon. Presently he said, "So they've connected me to the Florida thing."

"Oh yeah."

"I was trying to cover my tracks."

"I know you were. So were they. That's why they're figuring Baltimore for today."

Bolan cocked an eyebrow at his friend as he asked, "They're onto my timetable?"

Turrin chuckled without humor as he replied, "Your six-day war, you mean. I don't know about that, Sarge. I do know that . . . well, they have a big wall map in the inner sanctum. Little black flags are stuck in that map, starting with the thing in Tennessee last week, and one for every day since. The black flag is already up for today, and it's flying from Baltimore. They're calling it Black Friday, day of the vulture."

"Day of what?"

"Of the vulture. There's this legend from the old country about the feast of vultures—something about the last man on earth picking the bones of the dead for his victory feast, something like that. Anyway, day of the vulture."

"They're that sure I want Santelli, eh?"

"They're sure, yeah. Look, I hate to admit this, but I still don't know what was going down in Florida this time. I mean, it's a super-secret. Nobody talks about it outside the chamber. But it was big, it was very big, and I do know that every boss on the council had a chunk of it. Another quiet joke making the rounds recently says that there's a run on the Swiss banks, so many guys have been tapping their stashes to get in on Santelli's gold mine. Now those men up there are scared as hell. They're all heavily invested and it's going to hell under them. Their caucus went on all night. They were still in session when I left there at two o'clock, and probably still are. The vibrations I get are that it is not all lost yet. The Santelli investment, I mean. The drift is that they are concentrating on cutting their losses in Florida and hoping to recoup on the other end."

"And the other end is . . ."

"Baltimore, right."

"Is there a Tennessee connection, Leo?"

"I get that feeling, yeah. Santelli controls the whole eastern seaboard south of Jersey. He had pieces of the Atlanta action, I know for sure. And he lost a couple of fingernails when you whacked into Kentucky the other day. So you've been nibbling at the guy's empire, even before Florida. I think he's very much involved in Tennessee."

Bolan quietly inquired, "Any word from our man there?"

"I don't hear those kind of words," Turrin replied quickly. "The least I know about that, the better."

Bolan sighed and said, "Right. Okay. So what happens after you deliver the message to Santelli? Back to the headshed for you?"

"Wrong," said Turrin, smiling faintly. "Bite your tongue, guy. You're forgetting my unique standing in the outfit. I'm the Bolan expert, remember. And it's do or die in Baltimore."

Bolan was frowning as he responded to that. "That's going to cramp my style, Leo."

"Depends on how you look at it," the fed replied soberly. "We could work it out. To your advantage."

"I'd rather you just check out. Don't wait for Sunday. Are Angie and the kids . . . ?"

"They're safe, yeah. Three days ago. But I can't check out early, Sarge. You know that. Hell, I have a job, too."

Bolan stubbed out his cigarette and immediately lit another. He sighed and said, "Okay, we'll work it out."

Turrin quietly reported, "They're sending troops to Santelli. I don't have all the particulars, yet. But they'll be drifting in all day, from various places and by various means, and they're coming heavy. To do or to die. My official assignment is *consigliere* to the war effort. Which means that I'll be in Santelli's shadow, no doubt, most of the time."

Bolan grinned at that. "Trusted advisor, eh?"

"Yeah." The fed chuckled. "This is one aspect of the life I'm going to miss."

"For at least an hour," Bolan suggested wryly.

"Seriously. I love to waltz these guys around the track. And the bigger they are, the sweeter it is."

"Just don't lose the beat, pal," Bolan commented, sobering.

"The beat goes with the territory," Turrin replied, sobering also. He checked his watch and slowly rose to his feet. "I'm running short." He called forward to April, "Drop me on the next pass, honey." Then, to Bolan, "Don't wire me, Sarge. These guys are all jumping up each other's asses and it's pure paranoia out there. So let's keep it loose. I'll contact you, and we'll work it out as soon as they've settled me somewhere. For starters, I think it's maybe the hardsite on the bay."

"Arnie the Farmer's old joint?"

"That's the one. You know the way?"

Bolan knew the way, yes. He took a hard pull

10

at his cigarette and said, "The day of the vulture, eh?"

"Yeah."

The Executioner let the smoke go and watched it drift overhead. "So be it, then," he said quietly.

And so it would be.

CHAPTER 1

BACK DOOR

Leo Turrin was completing a hazardous personal contact with Mack Bolan, and was preparing to disembark from the latter's rolling command post, when Bolan's driver, the lovely April Rose, sent back a tense report.

"I believe there's trouble at the back door," the girl called through the intercom.

Bolan's eyes moved farther than his lips as he snapped back, "Read it!"

"I read it one hundred yards to the rear and maintaining through the last three turns. Large sedan with at least two radiating bodies aboard. Unable refine beyond that."

"Friend or Foe!" Bolan commanded.

"Tried it already," April reported. "Negative. No transponder response."

Turrin growled. "Dammit! They're on *me!* I'd have *sworn* I was clean! Dammit, I—"

13

"Local cops, maybe," Bolan suggested tautly. "Let's try some ears." He quickly fired up the war room's communications console and brought a pair of scanners on the line, at the same moment calling forward to the con, "Give us some stretch, April."

The big cruiser abruptly turned east into a subdivision and accelerated smoothly along a darkened residential street.

"Read it!"

"Target is slowing. Target is . . . okay, right behind us again and now accelerating. The range is one-four-zero yards and closing fast."

The radio scanners were revealing absolutely no activity on the police bands.

A moment later, April reported, "Target resumed one hundred yards and maintaining. It's a glue job."

Turrin muttered, "I told you it was pure paranoia out there. They must have tagged me at the airport. Now isn't *this* a hell of a mess."

"Not yet," Bolan growled. He gave the girl some terse instructions, then told Turrin, "Stay with April, Leo. If the worse gets worse, you know what to do."

Before the double-lifer from New York could even bat an eye in response to that, the big guy was at the door and the cruiser was in another abrupt turn, slowing momentarily. Then Bolan was out of there and instantly lost in the darkness outside.

Turrin's heart was hammering at his ribs as he quickly went forward and took the con beside April Rose. Completely erased were all thoughts of identity games with this lady. She was slowly bringing the big rig to a halt and peering intently at a reddish—glowing electronic screen, which was mounted in the cockpit. "The famous suck play," she said in a hushed voice, eyes still on the screen. "They're slowing. They're stopping. Target is at rest. Okay. It's okay. He'll check it out. If they're clean . . ."

His consciousness was dividing, part of it admiring the cool professionalism of this woman, another part marveling once again at the sophisticated systems that were packed into this battleship-on-land, but most of him just worried as hell and feeling miserable about the jeopardy he'd brought here. Not that it was anything new. Extreme jeopardy had been a routine way of life for both men for as long as either could remember. Eyeball encounters such as this one could do nothing but compound the dangers. There were times, of course, when the advantages of a personal meeting were felt to outweigh the risk, and this had been one of those times.

Hell . . .

The relationship with Bolan went back a long ways. And it had been a damned productive one, in many respects. Leo Turrin lived more than a double life. When Bolan had entered the picture, it had become a triple life— and there had been some outrageous times when "the life" seemed to expand into infinite partitions.

Though a blood nephew to the late Sergio Frenchi, who was a founding father of *La Cosa Nostra*—and despite the fact he'd been a "made man" since early in his youth—Turrin had returned from military service in Vietnam determined to help break the invisible, but smothering grasp that organized crime was exerting on all of the nation's institutions. The federal authorities were naturally delighted to have such a well-placed convert. They had given him the code name "Sticker," a fitting tag since it was Turrin's assignment to rise as high as possible within the ranks of Mafia power, providing the government with as much intelligence as he could without compromising his position within the hierarchy. Which had not been an easy job, at the best of times. Then when *Bolan* came along . . .

Shi—i—i—t.

Leo had been a lieutenant, or *caporegime*, in his Uncle Sergio's western Massachusetts crime family—in Bolan's home town of Pittsfield. He had actually played a part, though a small one, in the tragedy which struck the Bolan family and brought Sergeant Mack slamming home from Vietnam.

That was when Leo Turrin's "life" had really become complicated.

For a tense period, during that opening battle, Turrin had been one of Bolan's prime targets. He'd escaped with his life only after risking it all to reveal his true role to the rampaging jungle fighter.

16

As a matter of historical record, Leo Turrin was the *sole* survivor of the Frenchi hierarchy, in the ashes left by Mack Bolan. For that matter, he was one of the few ranking men to *ever* survive an eye-to-eye confrontation with that guy. Moreover, it was another matter of historical record that the two men had worked together briefly in an open relationship during those incubatory days, before Bolan brought his war raging to the surface, and was meanwhile posing as a Mafia recruit in Turrin's cadre.

Talk about complications . . .

Not only did the mob want Mack Bolan's head in a sack, but the entire police establishment, including Turrin's own feds, wanted his butt behind bars. And both sides had immediately begun looking to Leo Turrin as "the Bolan expert."

Infinite lives, yeah.

There had never been a moment, though, when Leo Turrin was confused about the direction of his loyalties. He very deftly fielded all the demands from both sides of his street while walking blithely down the middle, hand in glove with Mack Bolan. And it had proved to be a highly rewarding relationship, entirely symbiotic to both partners. Each owed much to the other. Neither would have come so far alone, and both knew and respected this truth.

It had only been very recently that the official hand of Washington had reached down in forgiveness and recognition to surreptitiously stroke Mack Bolan's ruffled fur. The guy had, after all, broken just about every law in the book . . . many times over. What the government belatedly began to realize, though, Leo had known in the gut almost from the start. This guy Bolan was something different, entirely different. The world had probably not seen his like since the age of chivalry. The motivations of this superb fighter had nothing to do with any *vendetta* or revenge mentality. Bolan's commitment was much too wide, and far too deep, to be powered by such shallow preoccupations. The family tragedy had served only as a sparking, as an awakening to truth. Bolan was, to put it as simply as possible, a guy who could not turn away from that truth. He'd broken the law, sure—but not out of any disrespect for that law.

Indeed, Bolan had broken the law because he had seen no other way to preserve it for those who deserved its protections. Hell, the Mob was running high, wide and handsome— taking what they wanted when they wanted it. And he saw that "the law" would not or could not contain them.

Well . . . Bolan had an answer for the Mob.

He perceived them as a nation within the nation, as an *enemy* nation bent on the destruction of all the noble American ideals. They were using our own noble rules against us— and winning—but here was a guy who would not sit still and let them win. In his own way, he reacted. It was not Leo's way. It was not a cop's way. Mack Bolan was a soldier, and a damned good one. He merely did what good soldiers do when their country is in jeopardy—he went to war. And whatever anyone else might call it, Leo Turrin knew that it was a glorious war, a worthy war, a damned deadly necessary war.

And he was winning it, yes.

Unless . . .

April Rose was fiddling with the console controls. She flashed a sympathetic glance at her passenger and murmured, "Don't blame yourself. These things happen, Sticker."

"Not usually twice," the Sticker growled.

She was refining the focus of the optics system and "augmenting" the infrared with laser pulses. Fantastic damned systems, yeah. A hellishly red image was beginning to flicker from the screen now, the picture somewhat like that of a film negative weirdly lit from behind by red lights. The outlines of an automobile glowed feebly within that image, behind which the brighter negatives of two men were framed in a tight two-shot from the shoulders up, both heads turned to the right as though peering through the window on the passenger side.

This ghastly image had hardly resolved when bright red pencil-flashes erupted just beyond the window, two quick pulses which streaked across the viewscreen to terminate at each human skull, jerking both of them into a sudden displacement down and away.

April's own head jerked slightly in empathetic reaction, and she let out a soft little sigh.

Turrin squeezed the girl's shoulder, muttered, "Hang tough, kid," and went out of there.

He met his pal the warrior at about the halfway mark along the dark street and told him, quite humbly, "I'm sorry, Sarge."

"Not as sorry as them," Bolan replied in a matter-of-fact tone. He was removing a strange-looking silencer from his Beretta pistol—one of his own developments, no doubt.

"Them who?"

"Ike and Mike Baldaserra. What's their connection, these days?"

Turrin whistled softly and said, "I dunno. Last I heard of those two, they were doing time in Atlanta."

Bolan agreed with that. "That's my make, too. Maybe you could find out, very discreetly, who's sponsoring them and why they tailed you from New York."

"Did they do that?" Turrin inquired with a sigh.

"The airline stubs in Mike's pocket make it look that way. And the car is an airport Avis. That doesn't read like a direct local conection. Do you think?"

Turrin shook his head and said, "Guess not. Damn. Well, maybe that's a blessing. Or maybe it's not."

"Depends on what you like the best," Bolan agreed.

"You're thinking maybe I've blown the cover?"

Bolan shrugged. "Possibly. Maybe you should safe it, anyway. Check out, Leo."

"No way," Turrin muttered.

"Stubborn," Bolan said quietly. "The guy is just plain stubborn as a damned old mule."

"Look who's talking stubborn," Turrin growled. "Second mile, for Christ's sake. Imagine that. A second goddam mile."

Bolan grinned and said, "Watch the swinger, pal."

"Same to you."

"Need help with the garbage?"

"I'll manage. Sarge . . . dammit . . . be careful. And sit tight till I hit your floater. Wait for me. Say you'll wait."

"Let's say I'll try," Bolan replied soberly. His eyes flashed toward the death car. "Sometimes you just can't, you know."

Turrin said, "Yeah. I know."

Those eyes flashed something very intense from very deep inside, then the big guy spun on his toes and trotted softly up the street toward his cruiser.

Some kind of damned guy, yeah.

Turrin threw a kiss at the night, and went on to take care of his garbage detail. He would do what had to be done, then leave that vehicle within walking distance of his own rented wheels.

"I know," he told the darkness. "Sometimes, yeah, you just can't wait."

CHAPTER 2

READINGS

"Good work," Bolan said to April Rose as he joined her at the con.

The girl accepted the quiet praise without comment. She turned the cruiser about and headed it toward the highway. The other vehicle had already departed the scene. When they reached Highway 2, Bolan growled, "Head north."

By the time she executed the corner, Leo Turrin's confiscated wheels were far ahead. "Track or break?" she inquired softly.

"Break," Bolan replied, sighing.

The girl sighed also as she moved to break the electronic lock on the disappearing "target" vehicle. The big grim man beside her was, at his most talkative, not your standard conversational item. At times like this, he was a veritable Sphinx. April had always tried to respect his mental privacy, but it could be aggravating as hell, sometimes.

After about six blocks of total silence, she quietly invaded that grim atmosphere. "Read it, soldier," she said, trying to mimic his command voice.

Bolan's troubled gaze met hers in the mirror as he replied, "I'm trying."

"Let's try together. Who got killed?"

He lit a cigarette and responded in a musing tone. "Couple of old pros from Brooklyn. The Baldaserra brothers. Torture freaks, hit men. For pay."

April made a face and said, "Ugh."

"Yeah. They were originally made by the old Mavnarola family. That's also the family that brought us such stellar citizens as Augie Marinello and Freddie Gambella. The Baldaserras went free lance a few years ago . . . I guess trying to revive a little Murder Incorporated shop for the New York territories. That was before I came onto the scene. By the time I first got to New York, the feds already had those boys on jury-tampering charges. We never met. Until just now."

April was clearly impressed by Bolan's phenomenal memory. She asked, "How do you keep all this stuff in your head? You're saying you saw them for the first time, in the dark, just a quick glimpse . . . and that was enough? You made them, then blew them away?" She snapped her fingers. "Just like that? What—from

24

some dingy old mug shots in your hinky-dink machine?"

She was referring to his microfilm library in the intelligence console, a thorough study of the denizens and habitats of the species *Mafiosi carnivoris*.

"I keep it updated," he replied quietly. "I can tell you what those guys like for breakfast. And I'd recognize any of them in hell."

The girl shivered slightly and wondered, in a lighter tone, "Are we away clean?"

"I think so," Bolan replied soberly. "Rented car. No radio. It's unlikely that they could have flashed any reports without losing the track. No, I think it's clean. For us, anyway. Sticker, now, I don't . . ."

"He thinks he led them here."

"He did. Which means that someone is beginning to wonder about Sticker."

"Sticker is really Leopold Turrin, isn't he?" she quietly ventured.

"Bite your lip," he said, just as quietly. "How'd you know?"

She tossed her head and said, "I look at pictures, too, you know. And I had a special interest. He used to have the pussy franchise in Pittsfield."

Bolan grinned, a bit self-consciously—his usual reaction to her use of vulgarisms. She knew that it both amused and slightly embarrassed him. Which was primarily why April did it.

He told her, now, "Leo had a lot more than that in Pittsfield. He had the keys to the kingdom."

"What happened to them?"

"I guess I broke his lock."

"I see." After a moment of silence, she prodded on. "I'm surprised you didn't break his head. Instead, you convinced him that he should come over with the good guys. I find it very strange." Another brief silence, then, "I've been doing some studying myself, the past couple of days. I've, uh, learned who *Cindy* is." She glanced at him. "The girl who sent you the annotated copy of *Don Quixote* when you were in Vietnam. With love forever. I was jealous of her. Well, just a bit. Then Mr. Brognola told me that Cindy was your kid sister, that she was dead now, and . . . and all about that. That's why I find it so strange about Leopold Turrin. I mean, all that mess is what started you off. And Leopold Turrin was the man directly responsible for it. Why . . . what . . . how did you get so damned big-hearted as to let him off when . . . when . . . well, it's kind of weird and I guess I don't understand it. Everyone in Brognola's shop knows that you and Sticker are thicker than molasses. I just never would have dreamed that Sticker and Turrin are one and the same. I mean, of all people . . ."

Very quietly, Bolan told her, "You don't have all the facts, April. In the first place, I did not convert Leo to anything. He was 'Sticker' long before I came on the scene. And he was not responsible for what happened in Pittsfield. Actually he crutched the situation all he could. Took some great risks doing it, too. I didn't know about that, at first. Something else I did not know, then, was that Leo was covertly helping *me* all he could, too. All the while I was trying to whack the guy. Damned near did. If it hadn't been for . . ." He took a deep breath. "We're thick, yeah. Leo is the best friend and the largest man I've ever known." He threw the girl an oblique glance. "Try to understand this: I'd die for that guy, with no regrets."

She murmured, "I'll try to understand that."

"And I'm very concerned about his present situation."

"Exactly what is the situation?"

"That's what I'm trying to read."

"We were reading together. Remember?"

Bolan gave her the information that Leo had brought from New York, concluding with, "So that's the way it lies at the moment, and I haven't the gleam of an idea as to what Leo is heading into. Hell of it is, neither does he."

"Well, he's a good game player," she said, trying to sound reassuring.

"Uh-huh."

"What do you *think* he's heading into?"

Bolan raised his hands to shoulder level and dropped them into his lap. "Who knows?" he muttered. "We're not dealing with—standard logic doesn't work, with these people."

"What kind of logic does work?" she asked.

"Crazy," he said quietly.

"Crazy logic?"

"Uh-huh."

"You're saying they're all insane."

"Of course, they're insane."

"Wow. You'd make a good witness for the defense."

It came out with strong sarcasm, though she'd not really intended it that way.

But he let it ride. "Who's taking them to court?" he responded softly.

"Right, right. I keep forgetting that you are the judge and the jury." She was trying to lighten it up, but—she knew—only making it worse. "I didn't mean that the way it sounded. I'm sorry."

Bolan was not rising to the unintended bait, anyway. He said, "I've never considered myself the judge or the jury."

"What are you, then?"

"I'm the judgment," he said softly.

Right. Right. A small distinction with a great difference. He did not judge them. They judged themselves, by their actions. Mack Bolan was nothing but the Executioner. "Some day I'll want you to explain that to me," she said quietly.

"You're the scientist," he replied. "You could explain it to me better."

"Action, reaction," she said, almost smiling.

"If you say so."

"So what about the crazy logic?"

Bolan frowned. "It isn't crazy to them. A twisted view makes for a twisted world. In a twisted world, smart is dumb and good is bad."

"So how are you reading their view of Baltimore?"

He said, "The men in New York could be thinking of cutting *all* their losses, with Leo as the pigeon. That's the way they would do it. Every move in a twisted world is a twisted move. And, yes, that's how they'd do it. Send an ambassador down to lull the guy into a false sense of security. Then pull the string on him. Of course, the ambassador doesn't know that the twist is on. Couldn't have that. Because when the string is pulled, the ambassador goes down the chute with everything else."

"Would that explain the Baldaserras?"

"Sure would. If that *is* the show New York has in mind, the Baldaserra boys would be the wires on Leo—their only job to keep him in sight and report his movements. With great stealth. Not because Leo is suspect, but because he has been dispatched on a delicate mission . . . and because the timing is very important to this particular type of treachery."

"Is that the only scenario?"

Bolan shook his head. "No. It's also entirely possible that the New York bosses have decided on a strong stand at Baltimore, just the way Leo laid it out."

"Where would Ike and Mike fit into that sort of scenario?"

"One of two ways," Bolan explained. "Either someone in New York has reason to suspect that

Santelli will not go along—or else someone is feeling a bit uncomfortable about Leo. In the first case, they've wired Leo to get a quick feedback on Santelli's application of crazy logic. In the second, they're watchdogging Leo in case he's harboring some crazy logic of his own."

April commented, "It gets drearier and drearier, doesn't it?"

"Yeah. Either way, I don't like the reading for Leo."

"What happens now when New York discovers that their wires have been cut? Won't they suspect Leo of . . . ?"

"Leo knows how to handle that kind of problem," Bolan assured her. "Those boys won't turn up dead for awhile, yet—maybe never. Someone may wonder where they are . . . but wondering is not knowing. In a world of crazies, who's to know whatever became of the Baldaserra brothers?"

"So what is your final reading?"

"My final reading," Bolan replied, in a matter-of-fact tone, "is that it's going to be a damned long day in Baltimore."

"Or a damned short one," she said, very soberly.

"You can put that in your teacup and drink it," he assured her.

Yes. To be sure. April had already done that. And the taste had grown quite bitter. For everyone concerned.

CHAPTER 3

AT THE JUGULAR

The sentry was about an arm's length away, breathing very shallow, half-asleep on his feet and lost in some quiet reverie of the pre-dawn, hands in pockets, shotgun propped within easy reach against the stone wall of the bayside estate. Dim yellow light spilling from a corner of the house at the second level caught him now and then, as soft breezes from the bay shook the branches of a skinny tree nearby. Young, very young—just a kid. What did little boys such as this from the big city streets know of the loneliness of the night watch, or the hazards of innocent reverie at the edge of the jungle?

Not enough, obviously. Two others here, far more mature, had finally learned all they ever would about that.

This one was just too damned young to . . .

Bolan's hand stayed for a flickering second at the fresh nylon garrote, still coiled at the waistband; instead, he stuck a cigarette between his lips, growled, "Bang, you're dead!" and struck the lighter in the kid's face.

The guy just about broke himself in half trying to pull it back together, trying to seize stature and shotgun all in one motion and failing to achieve either.

He gasped, "Jesus! You scared the shit outta me!"

"Be damned glad that's all you lost, kid," Bolan growled, in a not unfriendly tone. "Someone else could've ripped your throat just as easy."

The young sentry tried to alibi it. "I didn't . . . I thought I heard . . . I was looking . . ."

"Forget it," Bolan said airily. "Nothing out here but you 'n' me anyway—right?"

"Right," the kid replied, obviously very much relieved by the other's casual manner. "To tell the truth, I been wondering why I was stuck out here. I ain't heard or seen a damn thing all night."

He was trying for a better look at Bolan's face.

Bolan obliged. Better here than somewhere else, with all the chips down. He handed his cigarette to the youth and lit another, taking his time and giving plenty of exposure. Then he told him, "Yours is not to reason why. Right?"

"Right, Mister—I didn't mean . . ."

"You call me Frankie."

"Sure. Thanks. Oh, and thanks for the cigarette, sir."

Nice enough kid. Under the circumstances. Under different circumstances, though . . .

"I said you could call me Frankie."

The guy was still off balance, floundering, uncomfortable. "Right, uh, Frankie."

"What do they call you?"

"They call me Sonny."

"But you don't like that."

"No, sir. I been Sonny all my life. It's time I made a name."

Bolan very soberly said, "I make you Pacer."

"Sir?"

"You wanted a name. You got one."

"Pacer?"

"Yeah. 'Cause the first time I saw you, that's what you should've been doing and wasn't. It's a name that'll stick. From now on, you're Pacer."

The kid was visibly affected by that. In this strange society of stealth and knavery, "making a name" was somewhat comparable to a christening, or a bar mitzvah. Didn't really matter what the hell the made name was; the important, thing was for a guy to have one, And only a boss could make a name for a guy. This kid was not so green that he did not understand that.

He gasped, "God, I'm sorry, I didn't recognize —there's so many people coming and going these last few days—I mean . . ."

"Don't finish everything you say with *I mean*," Bolan instructed him. "People will think you play with yourself too much. Whatever you say, say it flat out and don't be afraid someone won't like it. Fuck 'em. Just say it."

Sonny the Pacer smiled at that and replied, "I guess I'm kind of tired."

Bolan did not return the smile. "How long since you had a break?"

"Sir?"

"How long you been out here?"

"Since two."

"It's damn near daylight. You haven't had a break?"

"No, sir."

Bolan growled, "No wonder you're out on your feet. Who's your crew boss?"

"Mario," the kid replied with considerable discomfort.

Bolan quickly sniffed the scent of that one and tried for it. "Mario Cuba?"

"Yes Sir."

"Go take a break," Bolan commanded. "And tell Mario I want to see him out here in ten minutes. Right here. Ten minutes. Right?"

The kid was thoroughly shook up now. "Right, Mister Frankie—ten minutes, right here."

The disturbed young man picked up his shotgun and trotted away, heading for the rear of the house.

Bolan went the other way—making no attempt, now, to soften his steps—and encountered the final sentry at the opposite corner of the property. He halted, took a drag from his cigarette and softly called ahead, "Who's over there?"

A mature voice called back, "Jimmy Jenner. Who's that?"

"Mack Bolan."

"Yeah, ha-ha. What's up?"

"Nearly daylight. How you doing?"

"Doing great," was the quick response. "Already since two I laid three hot blondes, a Chinese nympho, and a spicey Italian momma. How you doing?"

Bolan laughed softly and replied, "Your dreams beat mine, Jimmy. Just do it with your eyes open, that's all I ask."

"You, uh—where's Mario?"

"That's what I'd like to know. I'm going to take some ass from that boy when I find him. Sonny says he hasn't been relieved all night."

This one was growing quickly uncomfortable, as well. "Well, it's not all that . . . uh . . . Mario's been out a couple of times." He was edging toward Bolan in the darkness.

"If you see 'im again, you tell 'im Frankie's looking for him."

The sentry halted abruptly. Bolan could feel those eyes straining toward him across the darkened yard. They were perhaps twenty yards apart.

"Are you Frankie from New York?"

"I'm Frankie and I'm from New York," Bolan called back easily.

"Well, Jesus! I didn't think I'd ever—I heard

35

a lot about you, Frankie. I had a cousin with the Talifero brothers, once."

"What's his name?"

"His name was—they called him Charlie Wonder."

Uh-huh. And the Taliferos had once been Lord High Enforcers of the national ruling council.

Bolan told Charlie Wonder's cousin, "Too bad about Charlie. He was a hell of a wheelman."

"Yes, sir, he was."

"Too bad about the Talifero boys."

"Yes, sir, that's awful. Well, that's the way it goes." The guy was a philosopher, no less. "That's the business."

Yes, it certainly was. It was also "the business" when the brotherhood's greatest enemy could walk casually among them, command them, and run them around his own track, break bread with them and join their secret parleys, and even build a reputation among them as "Frankie," the hottest gun in the east.

This guy had evidently decided to venture no closer to the hotshot from the headshed.

Bolan told him, "You stick right there until I say different."

"Yes, sir, I been sticking right here since two. I'm here till six."

"Wrong, Jimmy. You're there until Frankie tells you different. You reading me?"

"I'm reading you, Frankie."

The tone of that troubled voice told clearly,

also, that Jimmy Jenner was trying to read a lot more than that.

"And if you see Mario, you tell him I'm looking for him."

Bolan was moving off, retracing his steps. The guy called after him, "What's going down, Frankie?"

"More than you want to know," Bolan-Frankie called back. "You just stick."

"Hell, I'm sticking," was the faint response.

Bolan did not doubt that for a moment. Sonny the Pacer and Jimmy Jenner could possibly be of some future use in this daring penetration of the enemy stronghold; for that reason, alone, they were alive and well.

And their chances for staying that way were, after all, about as good as Bolan's. He had not waited for Leo Turrin's "contact." It was Friday. Someone was planning a feast. And Bolan did not intend that they pick their teeth with Leo's bones. He had opted for a damned short day. And he was going straight for the enemy's jugular. Let the vultures take what they would.

CHAPTER 4

PRE-EMPTED

The old walled estate had been built some time around the turn of the century, constructed almost like a castle with a dry moat on three sides and Chesapeake Bay at the rear. It had been used by bootleggers during the probition era, had served briefly as a high-class whorehouse, and had fallen naturally to Arnesto "the Farmer" Castiglione when he sewed up the territory for the mob early in World War Two.

Arnie had "patriotically" turned the place over for use as a seaman's rest and recreation center, serving convalescing victims of the U-boat blockades in the Atlantic. It was no odd coincidence that the "old joint" soon thereafter became a thriving center for black market operations. With war's end and a dwindling demand for black market commodities, the old joint beside the bay was refurbished and converted to a "hard site," or militant center, for Castiglione's east coast ambitions.

A lot of shit had gone down there.

A lot of anguish, and a lot of agony, had filled those walls. And a lot of souls had been broken in the dank basement rooms, which had once been filled with illegal booze and contraband.

Bolan had not really assaulted this territory before, except for a couple of brief forays into Washington. His battles with Arnie the Farmer had been waged on other turf, and the Farmer himself had met death in the shadow of another castle, also renowned for suffering, in a distant land. But Bolan had seen this place before . . . knew its history . . . and its dangers. So he was not venturing mindlessly into some fool's game of cock and swagger. He was going for the jugular—and this happened to be the place where that was at.

Frankie-Bolan's fame had preceded him into the old joint. The guy at the back door was a slightly older version of Sonny the Pacer, and he was just a bit goggle-eyed to be in the presence of such a great one. The houseman did not know what to do with his hands as he told the impressive visitor, "I didn't know you was here, sir. I'm sorry."

Bolan showed that guy about half a smile as he replied to that. "You're not supposed to know, kid, until I want you to know. What're you sorry about?"

Those distressed hands became even busier.

"No, I just meant . . . I just heard . . . I mean . . ."

Bolan turned the smile on full force. "You mean no red carpet. Forget it. Where's everybody? Still in bed?"

The guy gulped and said, "Larry Haggle just got back with—uh, they went upstairs, I think. I guess Mr. Santelli didn't get to bed till a couple hours ago. So I don't—"

"Who's with him?"

"With Larry Haggle? I didn't catch the . . . a guy from . . . oh, did you come with? I—"

"Naw, who's with Santelli?"

"Mr. Damon's here. And Mr. La Carpa. They got in about one o'clock."

"With their boys?"

"With all their boys, yes sir. Full crews, looked like. We put those boys in the garage apartments."

"Feed 'em?"

"Sir? Oh, they got everything they need out there, sir."

"No booze," Bolan commanded sternly.

The guy was scandalized by the suggestion. "Oh, no *sir*, absolutely no booze, not at a time like this."

"Who's your house boss?"

"Carmen Reddi is the house boss, sir."

"What's the plan?"

"Sir?"

"For the day. The plan for the day. Does he know that a hundred or more boys will be nestling in here today? Is he set up to handle that?"

"God, I couldn't say about that, sir."

"Then you better go roust his ass from the sack and ask him. Tell him he should get with me if he's got any questions."

The guy popped his jaw and said, "Yes, sir."

Bolan scowled at him. "Well, dammit, go do it!"

The flustered houseman finally found a place for his hands. He jammed them into his pockets, and hurried away on his errand.

Having practically taken the joint over, Bolan went exploring. It had been a grand mansion, at one time, no doubt about that. Now the old joint was showing the effects of neglect and decay, indifferent housekeeping, irreverent occupants. This was not Santelli's home; it was his fortress, his hideout. Part of the downstairs had been closed off and was not even furnished. The rest was non-decorated with what appeared to be castoffs from Goodwill, that had been thrown together in a careless mismatch. Musty draperies cloaked the windows; the carpeting, where it existed, was threadbare. The exceptions to this neglect were the kitchen and the library, or what had once been the library. The former was gleamingly modern, clean, well stocked, the latter a magnificently decorated chamber befitting a royal retreat, containing an oval desk as large as a concert grand piano, a massive conference table fully twenty feet long with matching mahogany chairs, a massage table and small gym in one corner, in-wall television with huge screen, several leather sofas, and ankle-deep carpet.

This, Bolan knew at first glance, was the seat of Thomas Santelli's underground empire.

It also became quickly obvious why the rest of the house looked so seedy—Santelli probably very rarely saw the rest of the house. The office had its own exit to the courtyard, beyond which stood the vehicle ports and garage—beyond that, and clearly visible through the French doors, Chesapeake Bay and boat docks.

No, the guy probably rarely saw the rundown old house.

Nor would he ever see it again.

The late Lord of Baltimore was sprawled face down in a thick pool of blood atop his mighty desk—not just the torso was laid out there but the entire body. He wore socks and a black Oriental dressing gown, nothing else.

His throat had been expertly slashed from ear to bloody ear.

A small man with his back to the room was peering into an open wall safe behind the desk.

Bolan took in the entire scene with one flash of the eyes, and his Beretta was springing to hand before the full impact of that scene registered in his peaking consciousness.

The man at the safe was Leo Turrin.

Not a hair was ruffled on his head, nor was there any noticeable lack of composure as he turned coolly to face the intruder.

He sent a calm gaze up the bore of Bolan's

black blaster and said, very quietly and almost sadly, "You couldn't wait, eh."

Someone could not, for sure.

Someone, for damn sure, had beaten Mack Bolan to the jugular.

CHAPTER 5

TAILOR-MADE

It was a fresh death, perhaps no more than five minutes old. The safe was empty and the desk drawers had been ransacked, but nothing atop the desk had been disturbed except by the encroachment of spilled blood. It was as though the guy had been carefully placed there, then sliced like a sacrificial goat on an altar.

More than likely, though, Santelli had placed himself upon that desk—with a knife at his throat and at another's bidding. Perhaps the safe had been opened the same way. Certainly there were no signs of a fierce, life or death struggle.

Bolan growled, "Get the hell out of here, Leo. And cover yourself."

The little guy sighed as he said, "This isn't your work, is it?"

"Not my style, no. Someone saved me the trouble."

"So how do you know it wasn't me?"

"Not your style either," Bolan replied. "Now beat it, will you."

"Let's do it the other way," Turrin argued. "You beat it while you can, and let me handle the garbage detail. This whole joint could be ringing with anguish and outrage at any minute. Half of Tommy's boys are on the premises."

"I know that," Bolan told him. "Also La Carpa and Damon. Have you seen those guys?"

Turrin shook his head. "I've seen nobody but the kid at the door and Larry Haggle. He brought me here from town."

"Where's Larry now?"

"He's got an apartment upstairs. Went straight to the phone soon as we got here. He said for a hot parley with the rest of Santelli's lieutenants. Said I should go to the kitchen and get some coffee, than wait for Santelli in the study. *This* is the study. You may have noted that it adjoins the kitchen. I didn't want any coffee."

"Larry Haggle sent you in here?"

"Yeah. Does it smell to you?"

"Sure does," Bolan mused. "Who's next in line to succeed Santelli?"

"Not Larry, not by vested right. Tommy kept him firmly in place as *consigliere* and nothing more. He's a lawyer and dealmaker. Real name, Weintraub. So you see he's not in line."

Yes, Bolan knew all about Larry "Haggle"

Weintraub, and his rumored role as the real kingmaker behind Thomas Santelli. His connections were supposedly worldwide, centering mainly in the Swiss financial circles.

"I would guess," Turrin continued, "that it's now between Damon and La Carpa. They're the oldest and the meanest. Damon has the political muscle. La Carpa is the hardarm. The other underbosses depend heavily on both of them to keep their territories afloat. So I'd have to say Damon and La Carpa, yeah."

"Go find those guys, Leo. Look in the garage apartments. Act like nothing has happened. You just got here, and you're bored and looking for company. Santelli's still in bed, you guess, and his *consigliere* is tied up with something else. Let someone else discover the garbage.

Turrin smiled tautly and replied, "Okay. Sounds good. What are you smelling? Someone setting me up?"

"Could be, yeah. Someone with a very long arm."

"Like, maybe, an arm that could reach all the way from the Big Apple?"

"Like that, maybe, yeah."

"Okay, I thought of it, too. It's a classic, isn't it?"

"Yeah," Bolan growled, "and looking more like a masterpiece the longer we stand here jawing about it."

"See what you mean," the little fed replied casually. "So what are you doing? Staying or leaving?"

"Staying," Bolan said. "For awhile, anyway."

Turrin was looking his friend up and down, taking in the fancy threads and the silk handkerchief knotted at the throat. "Looks like you *came* to stay," he grunted. "Who are you this time?"

"I came *prepared* to stay," Bolan corrected him. He grinned, adding, "And you can call me Frankie."

"There's a winner, for sure," Turrin said breezily and went out of there.

A winner, maybe. And maybe not.

The almost legendary "Frankie" had achieved his underworld fame as a supposed "Black Ace" —one of the *commissione*'s top trouble-shooters, a man of almost unlimited authority and amazing abilities. It had been whispered that such a man could temporarily remove any *capo*, anywhere, anytime—that, indeed, in very special cases, such a man could "hit" any boss on his own say-so.

There actually had been such men and such power once. They had constituted an elite and highly secretive force, pledged to *La Cosa Nostra* itself, rather than to any family or to any *capo*. In effect, the Aces were the physical will of *La Commissione*—the ruling council of bosses—acting as a self-propelled *gestapo* in settling inter-family disputes or territorial squabbles that might threaten the stability of the overall organization. Theoretically, then, no one boss or family could effectively adopt open practices or procedures which had not found

48

prior approval at *La Commissione*. Nor had anyone better try anything under the table, either. The Aces were there to see that they did not—and the beauty (as well as the inherent weakness) of the thing was that nobody ever really knew just who those Aces were. Not even the bosses, themselves.

Hard to believe, perhaps, but it was just another of those insane twists in this demented world of *Mafia*. There had been a time, of course, when the top Aces were carefully screened and handpicked by the council of bosses. But the thing had gotten out of hand. Old bosses died and young ones took their places on the council. Some of those young ones had died, too, before their seat at the council of kings could be fully and unconditionally validated. There had to be a continuity of power if the organization was to survive and prosper.

Or, at least, that was the argument. By one twist and another, one old man had gradually and by conscious design become the only link between the council of bosses and the increasingly autonomous secret society within.

When that old man died . . . well, full autonomy became an immediate fact. For awhile.

The Aces were identified by a secret number and a code name, either of which could change, and did with sometimes astonishing frequency —face changes, as well. It was said that some of the older Aces had undergone plastic surgery so many times that they themselves could no longer remember who they used to be. This was said jokingly, but it was very close to the truth.

They carried specially embossed "markers"— playing cards sealed in hard plastic with code name and number indelibly engraved on the back, the suit designating rank. The Black Aces were, appropriately, in clubs and spades. Red Aces were hearts and diamonds. Red Aces could not interfere in intra-family business, except by prior consent of that family's boss. Only an Ace of Spaces could overrule, contravene, or "replace" a *capo*. A *capo* was a boss who also held a seat on the national council of bosses, *La Commissione*.

As savage and ruthless as this subculture undeniably was, it was also permeated through and through with a strange and curious code of ethics—a sort of natural code, a *jungle* code in which, just like with the lower animals, certain signals were continually being transmitted and received to establish at least a semblance of order and survivalist organization. These were "protocols," formalistic little rituals of the pecking order by which respect and honor were appropriately conferred. In a savage society, such devices were mandatory and dogmatically adhered to. Only thus could there ever be an organization of thugs. The men who fashioned the modern Mafia probably recognized this truth as a lesson long demonstrated within the bandit societies of Europe and the Mediterranean. Or, perhaps, it was just one of those innate, subconsciously realized survival mechanisms.

Whatever, the modern Mafia was ruled *in spirit* by an ingrained set of courtesies and formal protocols, which would be regarded as insane by any contemporary businessman or politician. It was this very "spirit" that had allowed the Aces to operate, and which, by the same token, had allowed Mack Bolan to operate upon the Mafia with such devastating effect.

The inviolable respect of secrecy, the absolute authority of rank, the unquestioned use of power, in whatever form, to gain a common goal; if these were the triune upon which had been built the fantastic successes and excesses of the modern Mafia, then they were, by the same token, the inherent flaws which could be operated by a wily opponent.

The Aces had not, of course, been regarded as "opponents." They were remarkable men, especially the Black Aces—truly remarkable—the type of men upon whom most of the Mafia myths had been based. Intellectually brilliant, physically tough, mentally persevering and resolute, dedicated, supposedly embodying all the deadliest qualities of the most persistent predators—and they were *loved* for that.

Indeed, in the most curious subterranean society, such men were idolized by the rank and file—and at least respected and admired by those in highest authority.

"Frankie" was, of course, an Ace of Spades.

There actually had been a Frankie, once. But Mack Bolan had come up with a higher hand . . . and had "replaced" the original. The role was tailor-made for a man of Bolan's measure. Under different circumstances, and of course with a crucial alteration of his basic character, he could have been a superb, bona fide Ace of Spades. So the masquerade, was a natural, easily assumed for brief periods. No one could get away with it forever, of course. But Bolan had often adopted the role of the Super Ace and had written new legends, as Frankie, in the Mafia book of myths. The whole thing had provided great service to his war effort—and had saved his life, as well, on more than one occasion.

Yet he had killed it all, almost with a single stroke, on a rainy day in New York, when the time had finally come to bury all the myths in a common grave. And this was, perhaps, the severing stroke, the killing blow which, for the first time, made final victory seem actually attainable.

Following that "command strike" at the Mafia's nerve center, there was no more autonomy, no more Aces in the original sense, no more tailor-made role for destroying the Mafia with its own insanity. He'd brought it all to an end, with his own fine hand, and in his own inimitable style.

All the Aces, Black and Red alike—those former "gods"—were now, as a group, the most hated and reviled of all fallen heroes, fearful of revealing themselves in any situation outside the confines of their own restricted power base in New York.

Except for one, perhaps.

Except for Frankie.

Perversely enough—or fittingly enough, depending upon the viewpoint—Frankie was the only top Ace to survive favorably in the book of myths.

Frankie was "okay."

Frankie had "tried to save it."

Frankie had "never betrayed nothing."

But how would Frankie fare in Baltimore? With a "replaced" boss on his hands and a do-or-die crisis looming at the horizon of the dawning day?

He was going to find out, damned quick.

Leo had been out of the room for only about thirty seconds when Santelli's head cock, the formidable Mario Cuba, poked head and shoulders through the open doorway to fix Bolan with a challenging gaze.

"Hi, Frankie," he rumbled, scowling. "You looking for me?"

The guy had never seen "Frankie" before, of course. But "the spirit" was working . . . for the moment.

"Hi, Mario," Bolan replied with ice in the voice. "Come on in. Get your ass in your hands. And get ready for a shock."

CHAPTER 6

BLACKOUTS AT DAWN

Mario Cuba was a human gorilla, a huge rock of a man who stood several inches shorter than Bolan, but who probably outweighed him by a hundred pounds or more. His balding head looked armor-plated, and the muscles of the neck and shoulders were so overdeveloped that the guy had to turn his entire torso in order to look to the side. For that reason, no doubt, he had developed a constantly shifting gaze, with the dark eyes probing continually across the full scan of vision allowed by the immobile neck.

The confrontation with his boss's dead body had no effect on that automatic routine, though the massive shoulders hunched noticeably and two great, hammy fists clutched the edge of the desk for support, or for comfort, or whatever. Bolan suspected for a moment that the guy was going to lift the whole thing and heave it through a wall, but then those great hands came away from there to fumble nervously with the waistband of his balloon-leg trousers.

The tortured gaze swept past Bolan a couple of times, then began a methodical sweep of the ceiling as Mario groaned, "Who did this?"

"Let's first ask why," Bolan replied soothingly. "That will lead us to who."

"Why what?" the gorilla rumbled, his eyes shifting even more frantically now.

"Why anyone would want to do this to Tommy," Bolan explained patiently, as though speaking to a child. "Who wanted him dead, Mario?"

The guy waddled over and hit the wall beside the safe with both big fists at the same time. The whole room shook and the chandelier swayed. He swiveled the torso for a scan past Bolan, then hit the wall again.

"If it makes you feel better, go ahead," Bolan growled harshly. "But it couldn't make Tommy feel any better."

Cuba turned about, shoulders slumped forward, hot eyes focusing squarely for the first time since he'd entered that room. "What the hell are *you* doing here?" he asked calmly.

"I was sent to watch the investment. I was a little late, wasn't I?"

"Maybe. And maybe not." The guy was becoming downright hostile. "When did you get here?"

"Get screwed, Mario," Bolan replied icily.

56

"You're forgetting yourself. Don't try to lay that kind of crap off on me.

That oversized body was deceptive as hell. The guy could move like lightning when he wanted to. At that very instant, he wanted to—and Bolan would have had his bell rung, for damn sure, had he not been anticipating some such reaction.

Mario was on him in a flash, those big meat-hook hands going straight for the throat.

Bolan went for the eyes, driving both thumbs in as deeply as they would penetrate, following through with a judo kick to the crotch.

No man is that tough. Eyes are eyes, and balls are balls, no matter who is wearing them. That mass of muscle went immediately to ground with a shriek and a groan, and it by God stayed there.

Bolan checked his five-hundred-dollar threads, straightened the neckerchief, and growled, "You fucking idiot!"

The guy started puking.

Bolan turned away from that, went to the door, and summoned help.

Sonny the Pacer and the rear doorman responded instantly, as though they had been standing in the wings and awaiting such a signal.

"Clean that up in there!" Bolan commanded. "When it's clean, come and get me! I'll be with Larry Haggle."

He did not await the bug-eyed acknowledgement, but went up the stairs two at a time.

The spirit, with a little help from the flesh, was working fine. And he wanted to keep the momentum rolling.

The door to the apartment was locked. It splintered open under a well-placed kick, and Bolan swept on inside. He found another exception to the downstairs decor. This room was all leather and chrome, with walls of books. The placement of other doors suggested another couple of rooms adjoining either side.

Larry Haggle was flaked out in a large leather recliner near the window, a telephone at his ear. He brought the chair abruptly to the upright position, gawked at the intruder for a moment of indecision, then dropped the phone and began scrambling to his feet.

Bolan opened his coat to display the hardware thereunder, and said, "Huh-uh."

Weintraub froze in an awkward position halfway between sitting and standing. "Which way do you want it?" he grunted.

"Suit yourself," Bolan replied charitably.

The guy sank back into the chair, but the eyes never left Bolan's face. They were the eyes of a legal eagle, a negotiator—a "haggler." This one was reputed to be the best in the business, his name, "Haggle," a tribute to that expertise. Forty or so, not bad-looking, lean and probably muscular—with a lot of energy suggested by the quick movements and crackling eyes.

"Who the hell are you?" he demanded, not really challenging, but not surrendering either.

Bolan approached the chair, and handed over

his marker for inspection. Weintraub took one quick look at it, then retrieved the telephone and told whoever was hanging there, "I'll call you back." He depressed the button to break the connection, all the while taking Bolan's measure, then quickly tapped out another call on the touch-tones.

"You don't mind if I authenticate this," he said, not really asking, flicking the ID card between thumb and finger.

"I think you always should," Bolan said mildly, return the direct stare of the lawyerly gaze.

The guy chuckled drily, and hung it up without receiving a connection. "Consider it done," he said. "I could've guessed it at first sight, You've got heavy guts, I'll give you that."

"Guts for what?" Bolan asked pleasantly, playing it.

"For venturing out of your kingdom. If I were in your shoes, Frankie, I'd damned sure have to be dragged kicking and screaming out of Manhattan."

Bolan said, "No guts to it. Just duty. Give me back my marker."

The wise-ass sailed it to him. Bolan caught the ID and returned it to his wallet.

"What *duty?*" Weintraub sneered. "I can't believe you guys. Nobody loves you anymore. Stay home. We get along fine without you."

Weintraub, you see, was not a brother of the blood. He did not respect the spirit. Bolan had to give him something else to respect.

"We don't work for love, Haggle. And we

never did depend on it to do our job for us. I was sent. Now I'm here. So wipe that smirk off your face before I do it for you."

It was a promise, not a threat.

The lawyer's face paled, but did not change expression. He came slowly to his feet, as though perhaps to square off against the implied attack. Then he smiled suddenly, reached for a cigarette, and growled, "Awww, what the hell. This is dumb, isn't it?"

"It is," Bolan agreed. "Especially with your boss lying dead right beneath your feet."

The hand with the cigarette froze midway between pack and lips. The guy was good, Bolan noted, at these quick freezes, arrested movements. Conscious maneuvers, learned for courts of law? Or a genuine mannerism, produced by stress?

"Say that again."

'Someone cut Tommy's throat. Not ten minutes ago. Mario is with him, now. But he's dead as hell, Haggle."

Some real, but indecipherable emotion briefly transited those inscrutable eyes, then the guy went ahead and lit his cigarette. That done, he said to Bolan, "Pardon me just a moment, Frankie," and went to his desk. He punched an intercom button, and very calmly instructed someone to "get up here right away." There was no acknowledgement from that quarter, but Carmen Reddi chose that moment to rap his knuckles against the splintered door and step inside the apartment.

Reddi was the house boss—the man in charge of security and housekeeping. This one looked more like a housekeeper. Well, actually he looked more like a headwaiter at an Italian restaurant—tall of stature, immaculately dressed in black suit, white shirt, black tie, dignified almost to the point of haughtiness. He was staring directly at Bolan until Bolan met that gaze, then it shifted abruply to the *consigliere*.

"Counselor . . . I guess you know . . ."

The voice fit the rest of the guy.

Weintraub's voice was sad, and a bit distant, as he replied, "Yes, I heard, Carmen, I heard." He made a placating gesture, sort of like a priest transmitting a blessing. "Look, I have to get myself together. I'll be down in a minute. Don't let anyone touch anything."

"Too late for that," Reddi replied. The cold gaze flicked momentarily to Bolan, then quickly back. "He told them to clean it up."

"Why?" Weintraub cried, eyes hard on Bolan.

"Because it looked like hell, Bolan replied evenly. "And because I'm taking charge of it. Tommy was a *capo*. We take care of our own." The cold gaze shifted to the house boss. "That's more than Carmen can say."

The guy flinched as though Bolan had sent him a physical blow. But the voice was cool and calm as he inquired, "What do we do with him, Frankie?"

No argument from the house boss, then.

Frankie was in charge.

"Clean him and dress him. Then put him some place cool. You have a big freezer?"

Reddi jerked his head in a curt nod. "We can clean one out. Oh . . . Frankie . . . I sent for a doctor. For Mario. Hope that's okay."

"A smart doctor's okay," Bolan said agreeably.

"We keep a couple of smart ones on call," Reddi assured him.

"How does it look?"

"How does what look?" Weintraub interjected. "What's wrong with Mario?"

Reddi spoke right past the guy, responding to the authority figure. "Hard to say. He's bleeding from the eyes. Otherwise he seems okay. Said to tell you he's sorry. He went crazy, he guesses. That's possible. He really loved Tommy."

Bolan nodded his head, and sent the guy a sign with the eyes.

The house boss backed out of there and quietly pulled the door closed.

Weintraub gasped, "For God's sake! *Mario* did it?"

"Nobody said that yet," Bolan snapped.

The whole thing was beginning to resemble a blackout routine from the old days of vaudeville. No sooner had Reddi disappeared through the one door, when another opened and a beautifully naked lady stepped in. She'd apparently just come out of a shower or bathtub. The blonde hair was stringy wet, and she

62

was still drying the luscious body with a large bath towel. She'd progressed to about two paces inside the room before she heard Bolan's voice, and became aware of his presence there.

The girl gave Bolan a horrified look, concealed herself behind the towel, and quickly retreated to the other room.

Bolan asked Weintraub, "Who the hell is that?"

The guy ignored it. He had something else still on his mind. "So what about Mario? What's wrong with him?"

"He went a little crazy."

"Yeah, but what's with the eyes? What'd Carmen mean?"

"Mario attacked me," Bolan replied casually. "Crazy with grief, I guess. You don't reason with a guy like Mario. I had to set him down."

"*You* set *Mario* down?" The lawyer's eyes went to the ceiling, and he threw both hands into the air. "I think *I'm* going crazy," he exploded. "I can't believe any of this! I guess I won't believe it until I've actually seen Tommy with my own eyes!"

"I guess nobody believes it," Bolan growled. "I've seen no signs, yet, of any excessive mourning. Except for Mario."

Weintraub fell back into the chair, and clasped his hands behind his head. "Can we talk like men?" he inquired, suddenly all cool and collected again.

Another court gesture?

Bolan took a seat across from him and replied, "I hope so. I got no time for little boys, Haggle."

"You're not apt to see a hell of a lot of grief around here. Not over Tommy Santelli."

"No?"

"*Hell* no. He was not the most beloved of all bosses."

"So what are you suggesting?"

"Are you conducting an official investigation?"

"I sure am, counselor."

"Then I suggest you talk to Damon and La Carpa. Tommy's greatest talent was his ability to manipulate superior men, to bend them to his own—"

"Like you?"

"Okay, sure, like me. From where I'm sitting, Talifero, you've got—"

"I'm not a Talifero," Bolan said mildly.

"Sure you are. That's a constructed term, not a family name. It means, loosely, 'man of iron.' I was using it complimentarily."

"I know you were," Bolan replied pleasantly. "Just the same, I'm not one. And I don't care to bear the image, even if you do think it's a compliment. The Talifero boys were pure garbage. They loved nothing but themselves."

"And what do you love?" Weintraub asked, leaning forward intently, as though really interested in the answer to his question.

"I love this thing of ours," said Bolan-Frankie. The legal eagle again threw up the hands.

"Uh-huh. So it goes on and on, does it? You guys have got to be the world's last romantics. Your damned *thing* is *dead*. Don't you realize that yet?"

"It's alive as long as I'm alive," said the "Super Ace," playing his role to the hilt. "But Santelli *is* dead, loved or not. Right now that's all I'm interested in."

"The king is dead, long live the king," Weintraub said, glassy-eyed.

"Something like that."

"Well, I guess I'd better go view the remains. Look, I'm not really all that—pay no attention to the way I've been acting. I don't handle grief and mourning very well, that's all. I'm glad you're here. Otherwise it would all fall on me, probably. That's good, you do it." He got to his feet. "I'll go down and, uh . . ."

"Who's the woman?"

Weintraub tossed an irritated look toward the offending door and said, "Do me a favor. Leave her out."

"I leave nobody out," Bolan replied coldly.

"Hey. Frankie. She's a piece of fluff, that's all."

"You know better than to bring a woman onto a hardsite, Larry," Bolan said in mild rebuke.

"Tommy didn't mind."

"And Tommy's dead."

"Well, hell, *she* had nothing to do—hey, she's a chick. Okay? She looks nice, she sings and dances, and I guess she's the best hump I've had in a long time . . . but there's nothing between the ears. Okay? She's a fluff-head. You want to talk to somebody, you talk to La Carpa and Damon. That's where I'd be looking. That's where I *will* be looking."

"Should I tell them that?"

"For*get* it!" the lawyer said savagely and stomped out of there.

Blackouts, yeah.

The "fluff-head" was none other than Toby Ranger, lady fed of the special projects group. Bolan had last seen her in Nashville, working the drug circuit.

The field of intrigue was shrinking so drastically that a guy could hardly put a foot down anywhere without stepping on an undercover cop. It was getting downright . . .

Bolan stepped into the bedroom, and carefully closed the door behind him.

Toby flung herself at him from three paces out, wrapping him thoroughly in sweet scented flesh with absolutely no insulation to cushion the shock.

"My God, but I'm glad to see you!" she whispered. "I think I've really done it, this time!"

What could she have done that she had not done many times already? The fabulous fed had done it all, *to* all, and *with* all. What could have her so lathered up now?

Oh.

Hey.

Yeah.

"You've still got blood in your hair, kid," he

66

gruffly warned her. "You'd better hit that shower again."

Blackout time ... sure. And the dawn had just arrived.

CHAPTER 7

MARKS

Toby Ranger and Mack Bolan went back a long way together. They'd first bumped heads in Las Vegas during the ninth battle of Bolan's war. Toby headed a song and dance group called the Ranger Girls—and they had been something else, those kids, taking by storm a town where talent and beautiful women were more staples in trade. They could have had highly successful show-biz careers, had that been what they wanted. It was not what they wanted. Toby Ranger, Georgette Chableu, Sally Palmer and Smiley Dublin were undercover federal agents, working a pilot program to determine the extent of encroachment by organized crime into the entertainment industry.

Helping in that program had been "the hottest comic in the land"—the one and only Tommy Anders (*nee* Androsepitone)—a very

funny man who made Mafia jokes on stage and
Mafia busts offstage. The five had proven to be
quite a team in Vegas. They'd been sent on to
larger problems, in other places. With Carl
Lyons, another old Bolan ally from Los Angeles,
they had evolved into the government's SOG-3
(Sensitive Operations Group #3), a daredevil
band of adventurers, who flung themselves into
one hot spot after another around the world in
the interests of America's national security.
They were not Mafia busters, *per se*. But the
mob was involved in many areas that lapped
over into national security matters. It was, therefore, not particularly astonishing when Bolan
occasionally overran the SOG's hunting grounds,
or vice versa.

After the Vegas gig, Bolan and the SOG had
worked together in a more or less symbiotic relationship in several other mutually interesting
operations—the latest in Nashville, where the
combination did a pretty good number on Nick
Copa, would-be heroin king of America. They'd
left Carl Lyons in Nashville, very nicely placed
in a crucial position within the Copa organization. It was one of the few times that Bolan
had walked away from an easy hit on a budding
Mafia boss, and he'd done so primarily as a co-
operative gesture to his friends in the SOG.

It was just a little strange that now Bolan
had been offered a secret appointment in government service—as head of a new supersensi-
tive operation which would, in effect, replace

the SOGs. He was, in fact, just two days away from becoming Toby Ranger's boss.

Of the original four comprising the Ranger Girls, only two were left—Toby and Smiley—which was not a bad survival rate, considering the territory.

But that survival rate was in danger of taking a sudden nosedive here and now, if Bolan's instincts were functioning properly. Toby had come to Baltimore via the Nashville connection. Apparently the harvest of drug market dollars being reaped by the Copa organization was being channeled directly to Tommy Santelli—or so Toby's group suspected. This came as no particular surprise to Bolan. He had already begun to wonder about the dimensions of the Santelli empire. A hell of a lot of money had been finding its way to Baltimore from some very diverse points—enough to make a guy wonder about the logic of that flow.

Toby had followed the flow from Nashville, and had, several days earlier, managed to wiggle her way into Larry Haggle's bed. Santelli had been in Florida at the time, and things had been relatively quiet in Baltimore. Until yesterday. The crisis in Florida had produced a strong local reaction, with much coming and going via car, boat, and helicopter. According to Toby's count, every major Mafia figure in the area had visited the bayside hardsite at least once during the early hours of Thursday evening. Santelli had not yet returned from his

Florida fiasco; Larry Haggle was presiding over all of the urgent conferences at the hardsite, leaving Toby pretty much to her own devices.

Santelli blew in at some time past midnight. There ensued a stormy, two-hour session in the study between the *capo* and his *consigliere*. At about four o'clock, Larry Haggle went into town on some unexplained mission (to meet Leo Turrin). At four-thirty, Santelli was still seated at the desk in his study, going over some papers, apparently all alone.

Toby could not recall, or had not paid particular attention to the time, when she next ventured toward the study, but the room appeared then to be deserted, and was lighted by only a small desk lamp.

"I knew that important papers were kept somewhere in there," she explained to Bolan, "because Larry spent a lot of time in there every day—'doing the books,' he said. I wanted a shot at those books. I figured with all the other excitement, I had at least an even chance to make some copies and get the stuff back before it could be missed.

"Well, I blew it. Someone beat me to it. The desk had been rifled. There's a trick panel in the wall behind the desk, hides a safe. It was open and the safe was empty. Well, I was standing there at the desk cussing myself, when another trick panel slides open and Santelli himself steps into the study. He has a small bedroom hideaway tucked in there. I didn't know that.

"Well, there I was. And there was Santelli,

staring at me like death itself. I was wearing nothing but a shortly negligee—comes just to the hips. I've found that's the best costume for nighttime prowling. If it isn't diverting, at least it's good for a variety of fast cover stories. Not many guys are immune to the suggestion that a sexy lady finds them irresistible.

"So I knew exactly what I had to do. It was all I *could* do. I opened the damned negligee all the way, posed prettily, and asked him if he was ready for his rubdown—made it sound like it was all Larry's idea.

"I don't believe he bought that—not the suggestion about Larry, anyway. But he was certainly diverted. Didn't even notice the safe or the desk drawers. But it was sort of dark in there, too. You know, spot dark. It's one of those small fluorescent desk lamps, hardly more than a nightlight, and—"

Bolan interrupted to ask her, "Could there have been a third person present in that room, Toby?"

She vigorously nodded the golden head and replied. "Evidently there was. All the time. But back to the story . . . Santelli just came over and grabbed me. All over. No class, you know. Vulgar. Degrading. I guess he'd poked and tweaked everything I have before I could even catch my breath.

"Well, so much for diversions. Next thing I know, I'm bent backwards across the desk, and the abominable wolfman is climbing aboard for fun and frolic. I asked him if we couldn't find some place more comfortable—hoping that he would take me out of that office and into the bedroom before he could discover the pilferage. But he replied to the effect that the sight of a naked broad stretched out on a desk always turned him on.

"So there I was, and I'd already resigned myself to another sacrifice for old mother justice."

"You weren't fighting him off?"

"Oh, hell no. What's the percentage in that? Hell, I'd invited it. I was going for *life*, Captain Thunder, not virtue."

"I understand that," Bolan replied mildly. "Just trying to get the picture."

"Well, here's a picture for you. Little Toby from Chillicothe is stretched out bare-assed on a cold desk and awaiting the inevitable. The lord of the manse is—"

"How was he dressed?"

She wrinkled the pert nose and said, "God, that turned me off even worse. I felt like I was in a porno movie. He was wearing *socks* and a flowing black robe. Now that's got to be—have you ever made love with your socks on?"

Bolan ignored the personal inquiry. "He didn't remove the robe, eh?"

"No. Why'd you ask that?"

"Still trying for a picture. Let's get back to the porno movie. The kid from Chillicothe is stretched out across the desk and the lord of the manse is . . ."

"He's kneeling between my legs, tweaking me and leering at me. Then—"

"He's on his knees?"

"Uh-huh. That's the way you usually kneel. See, you bend both legs and support the weight of your body on your knees. That's called kneeling."

"Sorry. No more interruptions. Go on."

"Well . . . he's kneeling there tweaking and leering. I don't know how long that goes on. I guess he's trying to get it up, or something. But then suddenly I realize that he has stopped leering. He isn't even looking at me now. He's staring at that damned open safe.

"I thought, oh hell, I'm going to have to kill this jerk.

"But it's as though he's forgotten that I'm even there. His head snaps around and he seems to be looking at something across the room, in the darkness over there. "Is the picture vivid?"

"It's vivid," Bolan assured her. "Then what?"

"Then the lamp went out. The desk lamp."

"It just went out? All by itself?"

"For damn sure, Santelli did not turn it off. Both of his hands were still on me. But the light went out. Maybe there's a wall switch. I don't know. I didn't hang around to find out."

"That's all? That's the whole picture?"

"Not by a *hell* of a sight. I was just explaining about the lamp. But the picture does get a bit dim at this point. I don't know exactly what happened after that. I know that I was lying there on my back . . . on the desk. Santelli was kneeling in front of me with a hand on each thigh. The light went out. Something hot and wet spilled onto my belly. I mean, you couldn't have spit once and counted to three between the moment the light went out and the first sensation of hot fluid hit my body. Santelli made a little sigh, and fell over onto me. The hot liquid was suddenly all over me and I realized that it was blood. I could smell it. He was dead weight. I guess I panicked a little. All I wanted was *out* of there. I managed to slip him aside, and roll clear. But his damned blood was all over me. I found my negligee in the dark and used it to sponge off some of the muck. And I made damned quick tracks to the shower."

"You just ran out."

"You're damned right."

"What'd you do with the negligee?"

"I cut it up in little pieces and flushed them down the toilet."

"That was smart."

"I think so, too."

"You're sure that's exactly the way it happened?"

"That's the best I can put it together, yes. Even for a pro, Captain Quick, that's a pretty damned unnerving experience."

"I'm sure," Bolan muttered. "Want me to leave it there?"

"Don't do me any favors. I'm okay now. Fire away."

He sighed, thought about it for a moment, then asked her, "How do you read it?"

"I read it," she replied darkly, "that someone wanted to get rid of the boss, and discovered the golden opportunity to put the blame on someone else."

"On you," he said.

"Sure. The perfect patsy. A lamebrain joy kid. What would I know?"

"You were supposed to go crazy," he suggested. "Scream and holler. They come running in and find you standing there with Tommy's blood all over you. Two and two makes four."

"Something on that order, I guess," she agreed.

"But then there's the open safe and the rifled desk. Evidently someone wanted more than a dead boss."

"I'm still working on that one," she admitted.

"And a small matter of the death weapon," Bolan pointed out. "I didn't see one lying about. And I looked for it."

"I'm sure it would have conveniently found its way to me," Toby said, "if I had hung around and waited for it."

"And the open safe?"

"That could have been handled, too," she sniffed. "What the hell is this? Are you trying to hang this on me? Why would I bother to lie about it? To you, I mean. You probably came here to kill him yourself. What the hell!"

Bolan nodded and said, "I did. But not that quick, and not that way. The man is not the empire. I want to kill it all. This is just going to complicate the matter."

"Well, don't blame it on me!"

"I'm not," he replied quietly. "I'm just trying to find a handle, Toby."

"Hell, I know that," she said, feigning a gruff tone. The dazzling fed lay back on the bed and tossed her towel aside. "See anything here you'd like to handle?" she inquired, still gruffing it.

"Four or five things, yeah," he admitted, grinning.

"But not now," she said, smiling up at him.

"Nope."

"Wrong time and place."

"Yep."

"Story of our damned life together, Captain Cautious."

"Yes. And isn't it hell."

"Do you think I'm dirty?"

"Sure you're dirty. But so am I."

She laughed softly. "Some men couldn't handle what I am."

He told her, "That's their loss. I handle it just fine. I put you right up there with Joan of Arc."

"Cut it out," she said, turning away. "You're getting serious."

"Always have been, Toby. You know that. I'd carry you through hell on my shoulders."

"Maybe you shouldn't." She was still looking away. "Maybe you should just dump me there. Maybe hell is where I belong."

Dammit!

It always came back to this! Not just for Toby, but for everyone Bolan had ever known in this lousy business.

Perceptions of good and evil, clean and dirty, were just too damn deeply ingrained in the conventional morality—and those conventions were too deeply ingrained in even the strongest of rebels. Those perceptions could not allow good people to do what they *knew* was right, what they knew was *necessary*, without carting around forever after a diminished view of their own worth. Sooner or later, it came to all of them—and it defeated a lot of them . . . even the very strong. It had come very close to defeating Mack Bolan . . . several times around.

He told the lady, "Hell is where you're at, Toby."

"Say it again, Sam."

"Every heaven is built in hell. We all have to build our own. And once it's built . . ."

"Yes?"

"There was a guy named Hubbard, a writer. He wrote something many years ago . . . I can't give it to you word for word . . . Hubbard said that God will not look you over for medals or diplomas or degrees. When you get to your heaven, Toby, there's only one thing that will pass you through the gates."

"And what is that?" she asked soberly.

"Scars."

"Scars?"

"Uh-huh."

"Gee." She raised misty eyes in a waifish smile. "I should be a shoo-in."

"I'd make book on it," he said, grinning.

Toby draped the towel across her shoulders and slowly sat up, crossing the shapely legs Indian fashion on the bed. "Okay. That takes care of 'poor me' time. Sorry 'bout that, podner. Where were we?"

"I was looking for a handle," he reminded her. "I was hoping you could hand me one, I guess."

"Sorry, I can't think of a damned thing," she replied soberly. "I realize that it sounds ridiculous, but I really can't. A man was snuffed with his hands at my crotch, but I haven't a clue as to who did the snuffing. Frankly, I was scared to death. I half-expected to feel my own blood start trickling at any moment. I just got the hell out of there."

"The room was dark when you left it."

"I'm positive of that, yes."

"You came straight back here."

"Uh-huh, as fast as my pinkies would carry me."

"So within a minute, say, after Santelli died, you were back in this apartment."

She nodded the gorgeous head. "Maybe quicker than that."

"Was Weintraub here?"

"No. He came in right behind me."

"*Right* behind you?"

"Maybe a minute later. No more than that. I

was just stepping into the shower when I heard him come in."

"So he could have been in the house when Santelli got it."

"I suppose he could. But I don't believe he did it."

"Why not?"

"Too messy, the way it went down. Larry is very squeamish about blood. I cut my finger yesterday—just a tiny nick, but it bled furiously. I thought he was going to throw up."

Bolan sighed and said, "Yeah, but necessity is the mother of more than invention. Other than the squeams, what do you think? How do you read the guy?"

"Ruthless," she replied immediately. "But he's the sort who kills by remote control. Like, maybe a thousand at a time with no sweat at all, provided he can push the button from a distance. I just can't see Larry rushing at a man in the dark with a knife in his hand."

Bolan said, "Okay. Thanks, Toby." He moved toward the door, then turned back to say, "Get your stuff together. I'm sending you out."

She said, tight-lipped, "Okay. Suits me fine. Everything here has gone to hell for me, anyway."

"What were you looking for?"

"The money wheel."

"You found it."

"I did?"

"Uh-huh. Tell your boss that Santelli was at the hub of that wheel." He sighed. "But it's bigger than narcotics, Toby. It's bigger than anything they've ever tried. Everything they have and ever wanted is riding on it."

"What is *it*?"

"Damned if I know."

"But you'll find out."

"Thanks for the vote. I needed that."

"I need something, too."

"What's that?"

"I need to be held. By a man. A *real* man. Just for a sec."

"Do I qualify?" he asked quietly.

"Hell. You created the role."

Bolan could understand a need to be held.

With no apologies whatever to April Rose or anyone else, he went to the beautiful naked lady and took her in his arms, squeezed her gently, stroked her lovingly, and did what he could to soften the marks of heaven that were upon that fragile soul.

Then he laid her gently back and went out of there, determined to find the marks of hell on Thomas Santelli's kingdom.

CHAPTER 8

STYLE

It had been about twenty minutes since the discovery that the king was dead—plenty time enough for the word to have been shouted from mouth to mouth all the way into Baltimore and back again. But the reaction within that hardsite was not quite right; something was missing. When a king dies, there is either rejoicing or wailing. Here, there was neither.

All the lights were on downstairs, and a dozen or so men were standing in the lower hall talking in hushed tones. Leo was there. So was Robert Damon and Tony La Carpa. A mean-looking guy of about thirty, whom Bolan did not immediately make, had a hand on Sonny Pacer's shoulder. The kid looked scared; evidently he'd been undergoing some harsh interrogation. Larry Haggle stood shoulder to shoulder with the house boss, Carmen Reddi. Big Mario Cuba was slumped onto a tattered couch near the front door. He looked a bit green in the jowls, and was holding a large compress to his right eye. Two hardmen stood with arms folded across their chests, backs to the door. Another pair stood vigil at the entrance to Santelli's sanctum.

It was a huge hallway, traversing the center of the house from front to rear, narrowing a bit at midpoint to accommodate the stairway, then widening again at the rear. All the rooms downstairs opened onto that hallway. The front part was large enough to be considered a room in its own right, forming a sort of lobby with two couches and several chairs, a couple of small tables, coat racks and so forth. Santelli's private retreat lay behind a pair of paneled sliding doors opposite the stairway. A smaller lobby stood at the rear, partially concealed behind the staircase, and serving as a "house station" or guard headquarters. The kitchen led off from there.

All eyes turned to Bolan as he descended the stairs. He halted on the third step from the bottom, very strongly aware that a hushed silence had also descended.

The atmosphere was not good—not at all good.

He made a little show of lighting a cigarette, and restoring pack and lighter to his pocket. Then he made direct eye contact with Robert Damon and said, very somberly, "It's a hell of a thing, Bobby. I understand how you feel. I hope you understand how I feel. And I hope you understand why I took it over."

Damon came right back with almost exactly the same tone to his speech. "Sure, Frankie. We all appreciate the fact that you're here in our time of trouble. I guess we're all just sort of wondering, though, exactly *why* you came."

La Carpa, the hardarm, was not quite so diplomatic. The voice was pitched in respectful tones, but edged very heavily on the downbeat as he amplified Damon's words. "What Bobby means, Frankie, is that we have just one question to ask you. Were you sent down here to do this?"

Bolan stuck the cigarette between his lips and left it there. His hand seemed to have hardly moved in the withdrawal from that action, but the Beretta was suddenly there where the cigarette had been.

One of the guys at the door twitched, but just barely.

Neither of the underbosses moved by so much as a flicker of an eyelid.

Bolan's gaze had not wavered from the cold clash with La Carpa. A little flare went off within those other eyes when the Beretta appeared, but the silence hanging there in the void could have been bottled and sold to funeral parlors.

Bolan very deliberately depressed the muzzle toward the floor and fed a round into the breech, then he descended two more steps and made a stiffly restrained little ceremony of handing the pistol over to Tony La Carpa.

"It's time to stop wondering," he said coldly.

La Carpa tossed a quick look at Damon.

Someone at the rear sighed loudly.

And suddenly the "spirit" was alive and well in Baltimore.

La Carpa's eyes warmed noticeably as he reversed the pistol and handed it back. "The wondering is ended," he growled pleasantly.

They shook hands and Bolan thought for an instant, there, that the guy was going to hug him.

Damon stepped forward for his turn at the hand, and the place began buzzing with excited chatter.

Someone said, "Frankie's okay."

Another exclaimed, "Did you *see* that *draw? I* didn't see it!"

It seemed that Mack Bolan was restoring a bit of style to this tattered mob. And none of these boys were slow on picking up on it. The entire atmosphere had undergone a dramatic transformation. The joint had come alive.

Bolan commanded the attention of the house boss to tell him, "Let's set it up in Tommy's office, Carmen. Wine and cheese and some good bread will be okay. Coffee, too, for those that want it. Enough for all the ranking men. We have important business to discuss."

Both Damon and La Carpa overheard that.

Damon commented, "Well, okay. A hand is at the throttle."

La Carpa added, "It's about damn time, too."

Leo Turrin had squeezed himself to the forefront to take that hand. He requested, loud enough for all to hear, "Include me in that parley, Frankie. I was sent, too."

Bolan squeezed the little guy on the shoulder and replied, "Sure, Leo, I was including you. I was briefed, I knew you were sent . . . and why. We'll be working together."

La Carpa exclaimed, "I figured it! Leo already told us about—okay! Okay! So now we know why!"

"Then let's pull it together," Bolan suggested calmly. His eyes again found Carmen Reddi. "Okay, Carmen?"

"It will take about ten minutes, Frankie. Why don't I just take everybody in? And we can get the kitchen busy."

"Do that," Bolan agreed.

Carmen took it over then, urging the crowd toward the office.

Bolan told the two underbosses, "Go ahead. I'll be right along."

Weintraub locked eyes with him for an instant, then smiled and followed the others.

Leo looked for an eye signal and received none, so he drifted away also.

The mean-looking guy with Sonny Pacer had now been made in Bolan's mental file as one Billy Garante, formerly a member of the palace guard under Castiglione. The guy had a harsh reputation. It was said that he had once been reprimanded by Castiglione, himself one of the meanest bosses ever, for excessive "discipline." Garante had beat a made man to death for stealing a bottle of wine from the royal cellar and getting drunk on the job.

Sonny Pacer had good cause to be scared.

Bolan stopped the two as they were moving toward the front exit. He said, "Hi, Billy. Long time no see."

Garante smiled, the eyes happy and a bit baffled at the same time. "Hello, Frankie. Glad you're here. But I, uh, don't remember . . ."

"Good for you," Bolan told him. "You're not supposed to. It was at Arnie's farm. Just before he left us."

"Oh." But, of course, the guy could draw nothing from that. "I guess you looked different then."

"Didn't we all," was all Bolan said about that. He put an eye on Sonny Pacer and said, "I need to talk to my boy here. We'll catch you later, Billy."

The guy was dismissed and he knew it. He let go of the kid, and started on out the door. Bolan called him back, as though in afterthought, saying, "We'll catch you right now, hold it a minute."

Mario Cuba was the only other man left in that area of the hallway. He was seated within easy earshot. Bolan placed a hand on Garante's shoulder and said to Cuba, "How is it, Mario?"

"It's okay, Frankie, thanks," the head cock rumbled, although the rumble was a bit shaky.

"Sure?"

"Yeah, sure." The left eye was swollen and angry-looking, watery. The right was hidden behind the compress, probably much worse. "Carmen wanted to send for a doctor. But that's dumb, I don't need a damned doctor. I'm just embarrassed, Frankie. I am terribly embarrassed."

Mario was from the old school. Bolan could understand his embarrassment. Junior rankers simply did not go around attacking top executives, regardless of provocation.

Bolan told him, "No need to be. Everyone understands. But I want you to take it easy for a day or two. Okay? Take it easy."

"Sure, Frankie." The guy tried a hideously mournful smile. "I'll be okay."

"Billy Garante here will take over for you until you're feeling better."

"That's okay, I can—"

"No, no, I insist. Hey—it's my way of saying I'm sorry, too. Okay?"

"Sure, Frankie." The big one slowly pulled to his feet, swaying slightly and steadying himself at the wall. "I guess you're right. I'm still a little wobbly." The one pained eye sought out Garante. "You come talk to me anytime you feel like you gotta."

"You know I will, Mario," Garante replied quickly.

But he probably would not. The guy was already beginning to swell with his new importance.

He asked Bolan, "Should I sit in, then, on the parley?"

"You should," Bolan agreed. "You too, of

course, Mario. I'll want you both in on this."

The two went off together, one moving painfully and the other swaggering with new-found, if only temporary, rank.

Sonny Pacer was waiting patiently for his moment in the light. Right or wrong, Bolan had to give him one. The kid was hardly older than Johnny, the younger Bolan. He took him by the shoulder and walked him to the stairway, then produced a money clip, peeled off two hundreds, and pressed them into the boy's hand.

"This is very important," he told him. "I'm counting on you to do it right. Do you drive a car?"

The kid was staring at the money. He said, in a confused voice, "Yes, sir, sure, I drive."

"There's a lady in Larry Haggle's apartment. I want you to get her out of here. Right now. Take her into town and drop her some place comfortable. Lay the money on her. For expenses, tell her. You with me?"

"Yes, sir, I'm with you."

"She should develop a bad case of amnesia. She don't know where she's been, or what she's seen or heard all this past week. That amnesia could save her life. Still with me?"

'Yes, sir. I'll lay it on her."

"Okay. I'm depending on you, Pacer. Play it straight."

"I will, sir."

The kid started up the stairs. Bolan pulled him back, and shoved another hundred at him. "This one's for you. Don't come back right away. Day off. Okay? Go to a movie. Pick up a girl. Make love in the park. Whatever."

"No, that's okay, Frankie, I want to—"

"Hey! It's a bonus. You can't refuse a bonus. I'm telling you to do it, not asking."

"Okay, sure," the kid replied, smiling suddenly. "I feel like I need it, anyway. I was on watch most of the night, and they worked my ass off yesterday. Thanks, Frankie. I hope I'm not out of line, but I want to say I think you're plenty okay. And I'm not the only one that thinks it."

"What kind of work?"

"Sir?"

"You worked your ass off. Doing what?"

"Oh. We had to load that shipment."

"What shipment? I just got here, Pacer. I don't automatically know about all these things. What are you talking about?"

"I don't know what it was, Frankie. Just a bunch of crates. Damned heavy. About forty or fifty. We had to carry them out to the dock. Took four men on each crate and there was only four of us doing it. I handled every damned one of them. Then we had to load them on the damned barge, too. My back knows about it."

"I'll bet it does. Where was the barge taking the stuff?"

"To a ship, I guess. Someone said something about the stuff going overseas, I think."

"You don't know what the stuff was."

"Naw. Just something very heavy. You could

ask Larry Haggle about it. He crated the stuff personally."

"Aw, some on. The counselor? Working with hammer and nails?"

"I swear. He wouldn't let nobody come near it. The storeroom has been off limits all the time I been here. I saw it for the first time yesterday."

"Where is that storeroom?"

"Downstairs." The kid grinned widely, and his eyes sparkled, as he added, 'They used to store moonshine whiskey down there in the old days. You ought to see it."

"We'll see it together some day," Bolan told him—lying, he hoped, like hell. "Okay. Go ahead and get the lady. Take her out the back way. Do it quietly. We don't want to embarrass the counselor. And treat the lady nice. She's okay stuff, too."

Sonny Pacer smiled and said, "Sure, Frankie," and went on up the stairs.

Which, Bolan hoped, should get a couple of worries off his mind.

The information about the shipment was very interesting. He would look into that.

First things first, though.

He had to bury a *capo*. But even that was not the first order of business.

Right now, he had to go to set the Santelli family's defensive strategy for a possible assault by their worst enemy.

Which was not exactly true, either.

Those guys' worst enemy was themselves.

CHAPTER 9

HOUSE OF CARDS

The long conference table had been moved up
to abut the oval desk, on which, less than an
hour earlier, the head of the family had spilt his
final blood. The death scene had been thoroughly cleansed, and Bolan could even smell the
lingering traces of room deodorizer in the air.

Carmen Reddi ran a clean ship.

Apparently the master's desk had been set up
for Frankie's use during the parley. Ten men sat
at the table, five to each side, grouped at the
end nearest the desk. Four of those were
lieutenants under Damon and La Carpa. Fault-
less protocol had been observed in the seating
arrangement: Damon and La Carpa first, fac-
ing each other: then Leo and Larry Haggle,
followed by the lieutenants, paired at their
boss's side of the table; finally, the head cock
and his understudy.

If that group had come from a deck of cards, the underbosses would represent the queens positions. Their lieutenants would be jacks. Larry Haggle would have to be a joker, useful only in conjunction with another power card. Leo, of course, was another wild card. As for Mario and Carmen . . . they were not face cards, at all, but highly prized "hole cards" of a value that couldn't be determined until it was time to lay the whole hand on the table.

Carmen stood stiffly in the background, near the wall, watching two of his housemen wheel in the serving carts. Those guys were more than waiters. Bolan knew them to be quite capable hardmen, though getting a bit old for the more strenuous duties of legbreaking and helling around, relegated now to palace duty and direct service to their liege . . . a pair of fives, maybe.

The head cock and the house boss held a rather curious traditional relationship, which remained more or less constant, no matter whom they served. The house boss was exactly what the term implied: boss of the house, which included everything under that roof from maintenance and housekeeping to internal security and bodywatching. In ordinary circumstances, he answered to none but the lord of the manse himself—whether that lord be a king, a queen, or whatever.

The head cock, on the other hand, was sort of like the captain of the palace guard, the hardarm serving directly the wishes and needs of the lord in a more military sense. He, too, answered only to the chief and was directly responsible for all security, and other matters involving arms and force *outside* the manse and beyond. In that sense, he was ultimately responsible for all offensive and defensive operations involving the direct desires of his boss, as opposed to those carried out under various franchise and territorial operations. The head cock was not in business for himself, nor was the house boss.

The division of responsibilities had never been written out as any formal procedure, but the roles were clearly understood and maintained by the pressures of tradition and common acceptance. There seldom existed friction or competition between the two, in whatever, famliy, even where the duties tended to interface or overlap—simply because, in reality, there was no overlap. Each man was virtually a sovereign in his own right, though faceless and technically rankless, exercising authority *in the name of* his boss in the area of his own expertise. There was no need to compete, because these men were as high as they would ever travel in their chosen field. They would never make a *capo,* nor would they even dream of such a thing—they were technicians, not business executives—and they would never become independently wealthy. But they would also never go hungry or lack shelter, and their positions commanded universal respect within the family.

But these two here, Reddi and Cuba, were now in a very curious position. Their lord was dead. In whose name did they now act? Whom did they serve?

For big Mario, the question had probably not yet risen to the surface of his thoughts. He was hurting, he felt humiliated, and he had not really been called upon yet to perform any duties since the passing of his king.

But Reddi, now . . . the house boss was undoubtedly very acutely aware of the problem. One did not serve a house . . . nor even guests in that house. What was served was the master of the house . . . and this house no longer had one of those.

But the problem went deeper than that even. One of these men now seated here would undoubtedly succeed as new head of the family. But which one? Not Frankie, certainly. Such things were not done—and, indeed, Frankie was a mere technician, as well. Frankie acted *in the name* of *his* boss—which was *La Commissione* itself.

However . . . that organization of bosses, which was headquartered in New York, would have a lot to say about which of these seated here would be admitted to their council of kings. Damon and La Carpa were not the only underbosses in the Santelli family; they were merely locally based and therefore geographically closer to the seat of power. Perhaps psychologically closer also, though. Still, other underbosses were scattered through the far-flung empire and although these were generally regarded as "colonials" it was still quite possible that *La*

Commissione would decide to sponsor one of those in preference to either Damon or La Carpa.

La Commissione was present at this meeting. It was present in the person of Frankie the Ace.

Some very important business was, indeed, about to happen here.

So, yes, many troubling considerations could now be working at the front of Carmen Reddi's head.

It was perhaps this inherent confusion that produced the only failure in the protocol of the moment. Thomas Santelli was hardly cold in his bones. No one should occupy his chair in a formal family sit-down, at least until those royal remains had been decently interred—in the strictest tradition, not until a successor had been properly chosen.

Yet Carmen had set it up as always, and there was nowhere for Bolan to drop his frame except in the *capo's* chair.

Or maybe the guy had very consciously set it up this way just to see how "Frankie" would handle it.

Bolan was not about to be sucked into anything like that. He positioned Santelli's chair at the left corner of the desk and sent an eye signal to the house boss.

Reddi understood that signal, okay. He brought over another chair and placed it at the missing boss's ghost right hand. Bolan lowered himself into the chair, gave Carmen a nod, and sat back to await the ceremonial "wine and cheese and good bread."

A houseman brought a towel-draped bottle and a large goblet. He poured a couple of fingers of wine into the goblet, and stood waiting expectantly while Bolan sampled the offering.

"It's fine," Bolan told him, returning the goblet. He silently signaled his desire that the sample be passed on around the table. That little gesture produced an approving flash from Reddi's eyes.

And, yeah, the guy had set it up that way.

But the ceremonies were off to a good start.

Almost. One of the desk phones rang. Reddi quickly stepped forward to silence the offender, then discovered that it was the "cool phone" which was creating the disturbance. Inappropriately named, the cool phone was connected to a national relay system, which very effectively scrambled both the origin and the destination of all calls passing through it. It was reserved for top level business only.

The house boss seemed a bit hesitant as to how to handle the matter. Bolan relieved him of that decision, scooping up the phone himself and responding with a clipped, "Yeah."

The cool system garbled more than station identities; it also produced a weirdly echoing distortion to the voices.

"Pardon me, but I need to talk to *him*."

"This is him," Bolan muttered.

"Thank God, I'm relieved, I was afraid— pardon me, I been on the run all night and I just now get someplace cool. Hope you don't mind me using this line. I got something really hot for you."

"I guess I don't know who you are," Bolan told those strange echoes.

"This is the one that caused all your misery yesterday. But I didn't call to apologize, Mister—sir. I called to give you something very hot in case you don't already know."

The guy thought that he was speaking to Tommy Santelli. But the one that "caused" the miseries of yesterday was now standing in for Santelli—which made this a mysterious caller, indeed.

"You better name some names," Bolan told that guy. "Don't worry about it. Just give me what you've got to give."

"This is the Pip."

Bolan's pulse picked up just a bit. Carlo "the Pip" Papriello was the head cock down on Santelli Island, the scene of Bolan's Thursday hit. Bolan had assumed that the guy was dead, or in police custody.

"Hey, that's great! Glad you made it, Pip. So what d'you have for me?"

"I think it was you-know-who, the bastard, that hit us."

"You mean, uh, the soldier boy. We, uh, made that already, Pip."

"Oh. Okay. I figured maybe nobody'd put it together that way yet and I—well, listen, that's not all I wanted to tell you. This is very embarrassing and I—well, I'm ashamed to tell you, but I think I have to and I'll let you be the judge of—you know, if I could make it up some way to you."

"Make it quick, Pip. We have something going, here."

"Oh, yes sir, I didn't mean to—"

"What d'you have?"

"I think maybe I got a make on that bastard. You know who I mean. I think he was passing hisself off here as a headshed Ace called Frankie. I'm almost sure of that, sir. He made a hell of a sucker out of me, I'm ashamed to say. He sent Guido away and put me in charge. What a sap I am. All the time I'm thinking he's acting in your name. I'm responsible for everything that happened after that, I admit it. I'm ready to take my medicine for that. But I wanted you to know about this."

Bolan told that guy. "You were right to call, Pip. We'll take up the other matter later. Right now I want you to take a vacation. You get my meaning. And I want you to keep quiet. This could look bad for all of us. And right now we have a very delicate situation. So you don't tell that story around, not yet. You get me?"

"I get you, sir. I'm really sorry as hell about—"

"Forget that, dammit! I'm telling you not to worry about it. Who else knows?"

"Well I'm in Lauderdale. You know where. Nobody's here but a couple of the boys. I'm afraid I told them, already."

"You tell them what I told you, then. Keep it under their hats for now. I'm depending on you to handle it. You and those two boys go take yourselves a little vacation. Go to the islands. Do it. Now I gotta go."

Bolan hung it up and pushed the telephone away.

"Turn this thing off," he instructed Reddi. "Turn 'em all off."

"Sure thing, Frankie. Uh, was that . . . ?"

"You heard, yeah, it was Carlo the Pip. He made it out okay. Poor guy probably crawled through the everglades all night just to tell us what we already know."

"About, uh . . . ?"

"Yeah. Now I think we better get on with this. Let's bury Tommy and get on with the business."

"We'll serve the bread and wine now, Frankie."

"Do that," Bolan-Frankie muttered.

And do it damned quick, yeah.

The whole damned house of cards was in grave danger, now, of falling in on Mack Bolan's head. A damned hole card had escaped the discard deck. And there was just liable to be hell to pay for that little oversight.

Maybe, yeah, he'd played his aces-high hand one damned time too many.

CHAPTER 10

BACKBOARD

The battle cruiser was parked atop a high promontory overlooking the bay. Innocuous-looking, sure—just aonther RV in the fast-growing fleet of luxury camping vehicles, which were quickly taking the hearts of freedom-loving Americans. But this particular RV was a freedom bus in the truest sense. For Mack Bolan, the Executioner, it was home—mobile base camp; weapons lab; battleship; scout vehicle; war library; sophisticated spy ship it was a one-vehicle logistics support unit for a one-man army; and it was the most impressive damned thing in Hal Brognola's long and varied experience with sophisticated police and combat technology.

But the wonder was not so much that the fabulous vehicle existed; the wonder was that it had been engineered and fabricated by volunteer help from some of the nation's top experts in the aeronautics and space programs: the damned thing had taken form in a matter of *weeks*, in the hands of less than a dozen men, whereas any comparable government-funded project would have required *months* on the drawing board alone, perhaps *years* in the final realization.

So that warwagon symbolized much more than one man's determination to crush the Mafia; it symbolized also the strong undercurrent of secret public support for this man and his task. Any of the engineers and technicians who had volunteered their involvement in that secret project could have been arrested and tried for high crimes involving the unauthorized use of highly classified information and materials. Some of the electronic systems in that vehicle were so advanced as to be at the very horizon of American technology—still in the test and evaluation phase in laboratories around the country.

In the final analysis, then, Mack Bolan's warwagon was the symbol of civilized man's determination to free himself from domination by savages.

Bolan himself had said that, though in characteristically plainer words, "Show a savage a bigger club than his own, and you can stare him right back into his hole."

And that, of course, was the sum of Bolan's mission—to make the world a safer and happier place for civilized men and women.

He had told Brognola, in one of those rare philosophic moods, "The meek will never inherit a savage earth. And, of course, the meek are the most civilized of us all. So they need a champion. They need a larger savage to stand on their side of the street and spit back. Otherwise the Huns will take it all over and we can kiss our grand civilizations goodbye."

It bothered the guy not a whit that many of those "most civilized" beneficiaries of his blood-and-guts crusade were sickened and repelled by his approach to the problem.

"I don't want their love," he once told Brognola. "Not even their respect. It makes no sense to take them into hell with me. They've got enough hells of their own to contend with."

A remarkable guy, yeah, on a remarkable mission—and he by God deserved all the support he could get. It was just a damned crying shame that it had to be *covert* support. Brognola would gladly step into the front lines with the guy. In fact, he had to keep reminding himself that they, too, serve who only watch and wait. Someone had to backboard the guy. And it had been only very recently that Bolan would tolerate even that degree of active support.

Even now, such support was severely limited by constraints which had been insisted upon by Bolan himself. Apparently the guy did not want to see official government agencies sullied or tainted by illegal and unconstitutional police methods.

"I can handle those scars better by myself."

He had not wanted to see the nation's watch-dogs became the savages—not even temporarily, and with the highest of motives.

Brognola sighed and stepped aboard the impressive gunship. April was seated in the midships cockpit, surrounded by a bank of video monitors. She had noted Brognola's approach, via one of those monitors, and had overridden the door's electronic interlocks to let him enter.

"Am I glad to see you," was her greeting to the chief.

"Came a'running," he grunted, "soon as I got your hit. What's happening?"

The girl removed a cassette from the audio console and handed it over. "It's all on there. He's wired for sound and the reception is excellent—really surprising quality, considering the limited power of that microtransmitter. Your technicians will have no trouble analyzing the data. You can even recognize very subtle voice characteristics. That's just the first hour. I have a new tape in, and the reception is holding beautifully."

Brognola frowned as he said, "You didn't rush me over here for a routine progress report. What's wrong?"

The girl removed her headset and stared at it for a moment, then replied, "Well . . . it didn't start that way, but apparently he saw an opportunity for a soft penetration. For the past hour he has been playing to the hilt his masquerade as Frankie Lambretta."

Brognola groaned and said, "God I hate

those. It's constant jeopardy, it's—every movement of the eyes and hands, every inflection of the voice is crucial. One false move and those cutthroats will be all over him. We wouldn't get in there in time to find a piece of his skin. What—"

The girl's eyes were sparkling as she interrupted that worried speech. "Let me tell you, he's a master. He *is* Frankie Lambretta, and he's got them all jumping through hoops." Those eyes clouded as she added, "But I'm afraid he's in for some real trouble. That's why I hit the panic button. I believe you could head it off at the pass."

What is it?"

Someone telephoned from Fort Lauderdale. It was a scrambler line. He took the call—posing, I guess, as Thomas Santelli. The microrelay picked it up fine, but you know how those lines sometimes behave. The voice quality is terrible. But I believe he was speaking to Carlo Papriello."

Brognola nervously lit a cigar while he thought that one over. Then he told the girl, "Well, yes, that could be damned big trouble. What's the gist of the conversation?"

She tossed that lovely head and said, "I couldn't be sure. Maybe your technicians can refine it some. But it sounded like Papriello was warning Santelli that Mack Bolan and Frankie Lambretta are one and the same."

Brognola struck the bulkhead with an open palm and exclaimed, "Damn!"

"But, of course, Striker took the call. So the cat is not out of the bag yet."

"Where was Santelli during all this?"

"Santelli is dead."

"Well, gee, thanks for telling me. What were you saving it for? Easter?"

The girl ignored the gibe. "It's all on the tape, you'll have a blow by blow account. By the way . . . who the hell is Toby?"

Brognola flinched. "What about Toby?"

"She's there, too. Or she was. Didn't you know that?"

He muttered, "No, I did not know that. Well what the hell . . . ?"

"Run the tape, you'll hear it all," April flounced back. "It's there in all its lurid—I can't believe a girl like that. I couldn't do it. And tell me something, Mr. Brognola, does every damned woman in the world have to fall in love with that man? How many more Tobys are there in the woodwork?"

"Not nearly enough," Brognola growled in quiet reply. "You're out of line, honey. The kind of love that passes back and forth between a couple of pros like those two is very much like the sharing of a life preserver in a shipwreck. So don't get your nose out of joint over—"

"Is it that obvious?" she asked, coloring brightly.

"Like in neon," he replied, smiling faintly. Then he sobered abruptly and told her, "Give me a line. I'll flash a pickup on Papriello. Did you say Lauderdale?"

The girl threw a switch and pushed a headset at her boss. "Yes, and it sounded as though he were calling from some location, which would be obvious to Santelli. He just said, 'In Lauderdale, you know where.' So if that—"

"It does," Brognola assured the lady. He donned the headset and climbed aboard that fabulous communications system.

Backboarding, yeah.

Hell . . . someone had to do it.

CHAPTER 11

THE ELEVENTH FACT

The curious thing, to Mack Bolan's mind, was that none of these men seated here seemed to be particularly concerned over the death of their chief. That little moment of tension out there in the front hall had provided the only real reaction, and even that reaction seemed to be bedded in jealous suspicion much more so than in any anger toward the death of their king.

Very curious, yes.

They had toasted the fallen chief, and symbolically buried him, when Bolan decided on a bold move.

He asked the question of none in particular: "Who sent for the Baldaserra brothers?"

And none responded.

So he asked the question again, directing the question to La Carpa, diplomatically reword-

ing the query, "Have you seen those boys lately, Tony?"

La Carpa spoke around a cigar, "Not since—
no, I thought they were doing time. Are they
here?"

"They were," Bolan replied enigmatically. His
gaze fell on Damon. "Bobby?"

The political arm of the Santelli empire shook
his head in a decisive negative. "Wouldn't know
them if I saw them. Heard of them, of course.
Like you."

"*Not* like me," Bolan informed him. "I am
sent. The Baldaserra boys are sent *for*. There's
a big difference." He moved the probing gaze
along the table to big Mario Cuba. "Mario?"

"Yes sir?"

"Did you send for Ike and Mike?"

"Hell no, sir. What makes you think they
were here? I guess I would've seen them if they
were here."

"When did you first see *me?*" Bolan asked
pointedly.

The guy dropped his gaze and played with a
fork, pushing down on the tines and rocking
it along the table. "So maybe I wouldn't have
seen them," he growled. "I was out in the
apartment for ten, maybe fifteen minutes. But
I really didn't mean me personally. My boys
are me. Nobody comes walking in here past
my boys."

"How many boys you got out there?"

"I got two at the gate. I got two at the docks.

112

I got two inside the walls, up front. And I got two outside the house, front and back."

"You dead sure about that?"

"Huh?"

"Have you checked them lately?"

"Not since . . ." The head cock looked at his understudy. "When's the last time you checked the set, Billy?"

"Just before—well, I was starting the rounds when all the hell came down. I run into Sonny Palo just outside the apartments, and he said Frankie was looking for the head cock. I commenced to giving him hell for being off his set. That's when you come out. I was up front talking to Jimmy Jenner, then, when the excitement broke loose inside here. But I guess they —well, except for Sonny Palo, I guess—but then I sent a boy out to take Sonny's set because I wanted to talk to that kid. Well, then—"

The guy had been speaking directly to Cuba. But Bolan took it up from there. "So you don't really know what you got out there right now."

"Well, I ain't eyeballed . . ."

"Not since we found Tommy with his throat cut, right in his own palace. Right?"

The guy's eyes were buckling. "I better go check," he muttered.

"You damn sure better," said Frankie the Ace.

Mario Cuba struggled to his feet, too, saying, "I'll go with 'im."

Bolan waved the big guy back to his seat.

"Jimmy can eyeball the set just fine. You stay, Mario."

Mario stayed.

The others had grown very restless. Fingers were drumming all about that table. A couple of chairs had been pushed back from the table, their occupants rocking rhythmically back and forth on the two rear legs. Leo alone was gazing directly at the man behind Santelli's desk . . . and it was a baffled gaze.

Bolan lit a cigarette, and let silence reign until Garante was clear of the room. Then he sighed heavily and announced, most emphatically, "The Baldaserra brothers were here. I saw them leaving." The gaze leveled on Larry Haggle. "Maybe you saw them, Larry. They were going as you were coming."

"You saw me coming?" Cold eyes shifted to Leo Turrin. "Did you see anyone, Leo?"

Turrin shook his head, looking straight at Frankie the Ace. "I wasn't paying much attention. I been up all night. Guess I was trying to cop a quick nap in the car. I saw nothing."

Robert Damon noisily cleared his throat and said, "You're suggesting, I guess, that one of us sent for the Baldaserras. And you're further suggesting that it was those boys that hit Tommy."

"I'm suggesting nothing," Bolan told him. "I'm just trying to develop some facts. So that you gentlemen can come to your own conclusions about this thing."

Damon bit his cigar and replied, "Fair enough. The first fact, then, is that Tommy is dead. The second fact is that somebody cut his throat from ear to ear. The third fact is that *you* discovered the body. The fourth fact is that both you and Leo, here, were sent down from the headshed, you say, to help us out with our Mack Bolan problem. The fifth fact is that *you say* you saw the Baldaserras here just before we find Tommy." The guy held up five fingers. "Now . . . is that all the *facts?*"

"The sixth fact," Bolan replied amiably, "is that the Baldaserras boys owe allegiance to nothing but the cash in their pockets. And the seventh fact . . ." He crushed out his cigarette and let his gaze move around that table. "The seventh fact is that Tommy is dead and nobody here seems to give a damn."

Dead silence again descended.

Bolan took a sip at his wine.

Presently, Larry Haggle released a loud sigh and said, "There's an eighth fact, Frankie, and I think everyone here will back me up on it. I mean, I'm speaking for us all. The eighth fact is that every one of us here, 'cept maybe you and Leo, were damned *glad* to see Tommy dead."

"Speak for yourself, counselor," Mario Cuba rumbled from the end of the table.

Weintraub smiled solemnly and said, "Okay, except maybe for Mario. But even he knew what Tommy was doing to the family."

"What was he doing?" asked Frankie the Ace.

"Robbing us."

"How?"

"Maybe you should ask the men in New York about that."

"Maybe I will. Right now I'm asking you."

"You want to look at our books?"

"I'd love to. Do you have them?"

"I have them," the *consigliere* replied calmly. "But you'll play hell seeing them."

"I guess I would," said the Black Ace. "Because when I walked in here and found Tommy, I also found his wall safe empty and his desk ransacked. So how do you happen to have them?"

Weintraub was still displaying that solemn smile. He said, "Push that button just under the lip of the desk, left corner rear."

Bolan slowly lit another cigarette, then ran a finger along the underside of the desk. He found a button and depressed it. One of the panels at the back wall slid soundlessly open, revealing a small bedroom.

"There's Tommy's hardsite," said Larry Haggle. "No windows, please note. Steel walls, Steel floor and ceiling. Automatic defenses right out of a James Bond movie. He kept the books in there. Everything out here is a damned front. The whole damned joint is a front. Did you know that, Bobby?"

Damon shook his head, coldly eyeing the little cubicle behind the sliding panel.

"Everything that was dearest to his heart, meaning his pocketbook, he kept in there. I even had to do all my own bookwork in there, and usually under his watchful eye. So whoever ransacked the office was just pounding sand. The heart of the empire is buried behind those steel walls. The whole damn room is a vault."

Bolan bent down to examine the pushbutton. He straightened up and said to Larry Haggle, "Damned easy combination, isn't it?"

"It's set for easy. I set it myself just a little while ago. It's got interlocks. I turned 'em off."

"Why?"

"Because I had to go in there and check to see if everything was okay."

"Was it?"

The lawyer jerked his head in a quick nod. "Everything in its place."

"Where are those interlocks?"

"Go to hell, sir."

The Black Ace smiled, and replied, "Maybe I'll meet you there, counselor. I was sent to protect the investment. I intend to protect it."

"So protect it. Leave it be."

"For the moment, I will," Bolan replied, smiling coldly.

"Fuck the investment," said La Carpa. "The point is, none of it belonged to any of us. We have no piece of this action. It was Tommy's own private little gold mine. And we all know damn well that he was taking from us and putting into this thing. Not only that, he was neglecting family business. My take is off by ten percent from this time last year. In real dollars, that's more like thirty-five percent. Meanwhile Tommy is running here and running there. If he's not in Switzerland or Germany or Holland, then, dammit, he's in Florida or California. While all of us are losing our ass."

"And we've been getting heat," Damon put in. "Plenty of heat, from everywhere. We're losing our faces right along with our asses. It's getting harder all the time to squeeze the juice or grease a fix. Just because Tommy won't stay home and tend to business. *Our* business."

A mighty unhappy family, yeah. And now it was all coming out.

Something else, too, was coming out. Billy Garante hurried into the room, his face all flushed with excitement and anger. He spoke directly to Mario Cuba. I got two dead boys out there!"

"*Where?*"

"The dock set, Nick and Willy! Both of them has got chokers buried in their throats! And they're cold and getting stiff!"

"Those rotten bastards!" La Carpa yelled, leaping from his chair—meaning, no doubt, the Baldaserra brothers.

Big Mario Cuba was also struggling to his feet. "Get a couple of cars ready, Billy," he rumbled angrily. "We'll run those cocksuckers to ground before they can . . ."

Now this was more like it.

This was the savage mob, snarling and mad as hell over an incursion into their territory, girding for a counterpunch.

But Bolan put a lid on that.

"Sit down, Mario!" he said harshly. "You're going nowhere!"

"Listen, sir, I—"

"I said, dammit, sit *down!*"

Mario sat down, the face going dark with repressed rage.

"You go running crazy now, and there might not be no tomorrow! You're forgetting why I'm here, why Leo is here! You put your ass in both hands and sit here, all of you, and listen to Leo! He knows this guy, knows his sets, knows what to expect! Now listen to him!"

Bolan got to his feet and caught the eye of Larry Haggle. "You won't need this, counselor. You come with me." He took the house boss by the arm. "You, too, Carmen. We've got to parley."

He took the two men upstairs, to Weintraub's apartment, and sat them down, then stood with his back to the door, arms folded at his chest. "So much for show and tell," he said coldly. "Now let's go on to the eighth fact . . . just the three of us."

"What do you mean?" Weintraub asked, a nerve pulsing in his throat.

"I mean that I turned the Baldaserra brothers away. They never came inside this house. They never saw or touched Tommy Santelli."

"So what the hell was all that . . . ?"

"Oh, okay, you're ready for the ninth fact, eh? Well, so am I. The ninth fact is that Tommy was killed by somebody who was able to walk

119

right up to him and lay a knife to his throat. Somebody who knows the house, knows the routine, somebody who knew just where to go, and when and how. I'm nominating you two gentlemen for the tenth fact. So now tell me how wrong I am."

Carmen Reddi became fascinated with the sight of his own shoes.

The counselor sat back in his chair and raised both hands to his head, interlocking the fingers across the forehead. Presently he sighed softly and said, "So why didn't you spring it down there, with all the others as witnesses?"

Bolan ignored that, for the moment. "What d'you say, Carmen?"

The guy did not look up. Like Mario Cuba, a bit earlier, he was obviously terribly embarrassed. "I cut him," he admitted quietly.

"Counselor?"

Weintraub let all his air out like deflating a balloon. "Okay, sure, we put it together. Had to. The crazy son-of-a-bitch was pulling it down around our ears. He didn't care. Had all his eggs in the other basket. So we put it together just last night, after we heard about the Florida disaster. You wouldn't believe—"

"I have no interest in your reasons why," Bolan commented coldly. "That's family business. Did you have a consensus?"

The two men exchanged quick glances.

Weintraub replied, "Not exactly, I mean, not specifically. But there has been a lot of talk that someone would have to do this sooner or later.

In that sense, yes, we had a solid consensus."

"Then you did right," Frankie the Ace agreed.

"So why'd you pull us up here for the private parley?"

Bolan shrugged. "You saw Mario. There could be a few others like him. I wasn't sent to save a *capo*. And I sure wasn't sent to save the whackers . . . or to judge them. I was sent to save the investment. Are you ready for the eleventh fact?"

"What?"

"The eleventh fact, counselor."

Weintraub sighed, cast a sidewise glance at his co-conspirator, and said, "I guess I already know what it is."

"Right," Bolan said. "So, now, why don't you just run down there and get those books."

The eleventh fact, right, was that Frankie the Ace was little more than a guided missile, remotely controlled from *La Commissione*.

And he would tear that whole goddamn place apart to "protect the investment."

CHAPTER 12

IN THE BOOK

Those were some books, all right. The most interesting set for Mack Bolan had to do with the influx of more than forty million dollars over the past several months, and a steady conversion to gold and silver—in bars and ingots.

Most of the money had come from mob sources throughout the country. But at least a fourth of it had obviously funneled in from "legit" sources.

Bolan could not afford to ask too many questions about that money.

He growled at Weintraub, "How straight is this?"

"Straight as an arrow, on paper," replied the counselor.

"How 'bout off the paper?"

The guy shrugged. "It would take a team of auditors and months of digging to say for sure.

I'd say roughly ten percent. A figure like that would appeal to Tommy. It's easier to figure."

"You're saying you suspect he was skimming off the top?"

"I'm saying I know damned well he was. But it's all very cleverly concealed. Phantom broker's fees, market fluctuations, and so forth. It would be a cinch to manipulate a ten percent skim."

"Then plow it back in, eh?"

"I think so, yes. As his own contribution."

"How would the books show that?"

"They wouldn't. Except that I know his income. And it's nowhere near the amount of money he's invested in this thing."

"You keep the income books?"

The lawyer nodded. "That's right. But I was never allowed to touch the other. Except for monthly reports to the investors."

"But you touched them anyway."

Weintraub grinned. "Sure I did. I didn't want to end up with red hands. Unless it was from Tommy's blood."

"You really loved the guy, didn't you?"

The lawyer sobered as he replied to that. "There was a time when I could have. All of us. But this thing made him crazy. Too much money here, Frankie. Just too damned much money. And this forty mil is mere investment capital. The return will be a hundredfold, maybe more. It made him crazy."

"I'm not supposed to know this," Bolan said quietly. "But . . ."

"I know you're not. So don't ask."

"But I think I'd better know. So I'm asking."

Weintraub got to his feet and stepped to the window. He gazed outside as he casually inquired, "What'd you do with my woman?"

Bolan yielded to that personal concern, though he knew that his hourglass was quickly running out of sand. "I sent her away."

"Why?"

"Ask Carmen."

Weintraub's gaze shot to the other man. "Carmen?"

The house boss spread his hands. "She was there. She saw."

"She was *where*?"

"With Tommy. I wouldn't have done it that way, counselor, if there'd been another way. But she walked right into it. I'd already opened the dummy safe and pulled the junk out of the desk. Messed it up good. And I was about to go take Tommy in his bed when I heard her coming. So I ducked. Then Tommy came out and started playing around with her. Well, really, she saved me a worse problem. We figured him to be asleep by then. He wasn't. So what the hell could I do? When Tommy saw the mess, I knew I had to take him then and there."

"Pretty damned sloppy," Weintraub commented bitterly. "After all our . . ."

"Right. But what could I do?" The house boss sighed wearily. "I was trying to make up my mind. Should I take the woman, too, or wait and check it out with you first? But she split too fast. And I didn't want to come up here looking for her, with Tommy's blood all over me. I figured we could handle it later. But then by the time I got my clothes changed, it had all gone to hell and I never had a chance to tell you."

The lawyerly gaze shot to Bolan. "Did she tell you that?"

Bolan nodded and lied a little. "She told me. And she saw it all."

"Well, then, where the hell did you *send* her. And *why?*"

"*Where* will be my little secret," Bolan told him, arching an eyebrow for emphasis, "until I report back to the headshed, mission accomplished. *Why* should be very obvious.'

"Mission accomplished?"

"Right."

"Meaning . . . ?"

"Meaning they want to see the books. You're not the only one, counselor, to wonder about Tommy's finesse with figures."

"Well, you're a hell of a guy."

"Thanks."

"Had it all figured out, didn't you? When you came down the stairs awhile ago, you already had it. And now you're holding an eyewitness . . . pretty goddamn cute, aren't you?"

"I try to be. It's a cute world, counselor."

Weintraub was mad as hell, in a slow burn leading surely along a short fuse. "How do I know the books will get there? Intact?"

"Money doesn't make me crazy," Bolan told him.

"That's right. I forgot. You do it all for that *thing* of yours, don't you?"

"That's right. What do you do it for?"

"I do it for this thing of *mine*," Weintraub snapped.

"Then do it. I need to know what I'm carrying to the headshed. Educate me. What's the investment?"

"The thing that makes the world revolve!" the guy replied savagely. "The chug and the choo, the woof and the warp, four on the floor, the thing that makes everything go, and all the factories smoke all over the world!"

"That's a damned long way to say *oil*," Bolan growled.

"Any way you say it, it comes out gold! And it's becoming harder to get all the time!"

"If you can't buy it, guy, you can't sell it. So where's the hundredfold return?"

"That's why guys like you are paid to kill!" Weintraub snarled. "Give 'em an order and they'll carry it out to the letter! Give 'em a portfolio, though, and they'll go broke in a week!"

"Then maybe you should explain it in words that a guy like me can understand."

"Can you understand words like *prohibition?* That's what *built* the modern mob, you know. Do you understand words like *rationing* and *scarcity?* Those two kept us going through the war—the *big* war, as they call it. Ever hear of big labor, big business, power politics—with everybody scrambling for the fastest buck? That's what pulled us through the postwar boom and expansion. Ever hear of *grass* and *horse* and *coke*? Those little jewels propelled us right into the Age of Aquarius. Hey, Frankie, the *Mob* is a *service* organization! Understand? Service! Forget all that romantic bullshit about *this thing of ours* and allegiance to the ring and all that crap! That's a con, to keep all the little people in line. We're running a *business*, dammit! Our business is service and the service is our power. The power comes from serving up the thing that every man wants most, or needs most, or loves most. We get shaggy politicians elected. We make labor bosses rich and industrialists richer. We make drunks and junkies happy, and we put a woman within every man's reach. We give a man what he can't get all by himself. That's not *La Cosa Nostra*, buddy, that's the *mob,* and it's *service,* and the service is *power.*"

"Oil service, eh," Bolan said. "Okay, fill 'er up. And check the tires while you're at it."

"Ha ha, that's very funny. A lot funnier than you realize. What happens when the guy says sorry, no gas. Check your own damned tires. I'm going fishing. What d'you say then? Do you say okay, I'll walk. Or do you go find someone who's willing to provide the service you need?"

Bolan was willing to play the game a bit

longer. He said, "I'm looking at forty million bucks, counselor."

"You're looking at a drop in the bucket, too. This is just the first installment. It just gets our foot in the door. Mark my words. The day is coming when gasoline is rationed again in this country. In every country, all over the world. And the price? Shit. You're going to see the biggest panic since the Wall Street crash. You'll see gas stations boarded up, and people lining up for miles at those that are not, just to get a few gallons of that precious shit, and to *hell* with the price. And listen. That goes double for a hard winter and a cold house. And d'you know why?"

Bolan shrugged. "It's not exactly late news, counselor, that there's an energy shortage."

"See?" The guy clapped his hands together and did a little dance in front of the window. "You bought it! Everyone buys it! Sure, everyone knows there's an energy shortage. You want to hear something rich? This so-called energy shortage is the biggest con since Hitler bought Germany. The shortage is in the books! Nowhere else! Any damned fool can look in the right book and see that! They got more *known* oil reserves in the ground right now than at any time in history. Keeps growing all the time. The world is running out of oil, *bullshit!* Hey, you think *La Cosa Nostra* invented the idea? Pull your head out of the damned closet. OPEC and the oil industry as a whole makes your damned *Cosa Nostra* look like a Sunday communion service. There's no shortage. Those sons-of-bitches will sell you all the fucking oil you want, anywhere you want it, if you make it worth their while. Hey! That's *our* fucking business, buddy. And we're going to get a piece of it."

Bolan smiled wryly and said, "Going to buy yourselves a sheikdom?"

"Naw. Not even close. We don't need one. It would cost too much, in the first place. And they're sons-of-bitches to deal with in the second. Who needs it? You ever hear of the free market?"

Bolan looked at his watch and said, "Just in case I haven't, tell me about it."

But the guy was coming down off his hormonal high. He dropped into his chair and growled, "Go take a night course. You'll learn that a hundredfold return is no idle boast. Maybe not right away. But soon. Soon. Maybe sooner than anybody thinks. Of course, it means nothing to me. I just created the thing. I got no piece of it. But you tell those gentlemen in New York . . . you tell them that Tom Santelli was robbing them."

"You wouldn't do that, eh?"

"I would not, no. A fair share would satisfy me just fine. You tell them, also, that Lawrence Weintraub is the one who put this whole thing together. Tommy took the credit, but I did the work. It's my child. I'm the one with the contacts. And I'm the one that set up the deal. So they might want to take that into consideration when—"

"I'll tell them that, counselor."

"Please do. And what are you going to tell them about Tommy?"

Bolan sighed and replied, "I'm going to tell them that Tommy was robbing his own family. And that his own family corrected the matter. That's all they need to know. It's all they'll *want* to know. After they see these books."

That disclosure revived the guy a bit. His eyes showed gratitude even if the voice did not. "What about Tommy's investment?"

"I'll recommend that they impose a ten percent tax and turn the rest to the heirs."

That revived him quite a bit more.

"That's fine with me. I have an understanding with the heirs."

"I would not," advised Frankie the Ace, "talk too much about that if I were you. Let's just leave it that Larry Haggle will be happy to continue on as administrator of the free market project . . . and that he knows he will be properly rewarded by the new management."

The gratitude spilled fully and warmly into that voice, then. "Say, listen, Frankie . . . forget all that silly shit I was spouting. You know," he chuckled, "about going broke with a portfolio. I was speaking from my ass."

Bolan said, "I know that. Well . . ." He stuck out a paw and shook the counselor's hand, then repeated with Carmen Reddi. "Don't worry about your books. They'll be in good hands." He was almost to the door, when he turned back, as though with an afterthought. "Oh, by the way, did the shipment get off okay yesterday?"

"Like clockwork," Weintraub replied happily.

"They may want to check it. You know, for confirmation of the books. And especially now with Tommy out of the picture."

"Then they better hurry." The counselor was checking his watch. "The tug was scheduled for twenty minutes ago. They should be clearing Hampton Roads before nightfall."

Bolan nodded and went on out, then came back again with only his head and shoulders inside the room. "That's the SS, uh . . ."

"Tangier Victory," said the man who'd engineered a forty-million-dollar coup.

"Right," Bolan said and went away without another word.

So.

Forty million dollars in gold and silver, eh?

So okay. It was shaping into a damned short day, indeed.

And it was time for Frankie the Ace to get the hell out of there.

CHAPTER 13

FATHER FIGURE

Bolan went by the boardroom to pick up Leo Turrin. The meeting there had disintegrated into factional powwows between the individual leaders and their cadres, huddling in tense groups at opposite ends of the room. Several new faces were evident in each group—crew leaders, no doubt, who'd been called in to participate in the discussions.

The atmosphere in there was nearing a flash point. Something was sour as hell, that much was obvious.

Leo was standing at the French doors, gazing wistfully toward the bay, a forlorn and obviously discarded figure as "the family" argued their "do or die" strategy.

It was not an easy job, his. The popularity of *Commissione* administrators had declined proportionately with that of the trouble-shooters, a sure sign that the organization as a whole was in disarray. Which was fine with Bolan. But doubly difficult and treacherous for a guy in Leo's shoes, even if he'd been on the up and up.

Bolan walked unnoticed to the little guy and asked him, *sotto voce*, "You ready to quit this joint?"

Turrin turned to him with a wan smile and replied. "If I could find a good enough excuse, yeah. These guys are all crazy as hell. I wouldn't be surprised to see them start shooting it out with one another."

"It's an unhappy ship." Bolan agreed.

"That it is. I, uh, figured you'd rather see them all mobbed up. That's the way I laid it down. But they're not buying that. They're just plain mad as hell that this *do or die* is on their turf. So I don't know. I get the feeling they're about ready to bolt and run, just scatter and lay low until the heat is off. I guess that's what I'd *want* to do, myself, in their situation. See, what the hell do they have to gain by standing? That's the attitude. La Carpa is the only one with balls. Even some of his cadre, though, is on the brink of revolt. He pulled 'em all to the other side of the room, and it's been fireworks ever since. They want to go with Damon."

"Where's Damon going?"

"He says Jamaica is damned nice this time of year. If New York wants to stop Bolan, then let New York come down and stop him. Better still, stop him somewheres else. And that's the prevailing wind, right now. These guys have all settled for small."

"You're right, Leo, I want them mobbed up. I don't want them scattering like cancer cells. I want them right under the damned knife."

"I don't know how you're going to get that. I've said all I can say. I had the feeling that one more word and someone would be tacking my balls to the wall."

Bolan pulled the Santelli books from beneath his arm and said, "Guess I better hit them with this."

"What is it?"

"Keys to the kingdom," Bolan muttered. He hefted the books in both hands. "Weigh about three pounds, I'd guess. Worth about forty million bucks."

"Solid gold, I presume."

"You hit it, pal. And a lot of it came from their own sweat. But they're not cut in."

"No wonder they're pissed!"

"Yeah. Okay. Let's get them really pissed ... something to fight for ... or to fight *over*."

"I'd bet for *over*," Turrin replied nervously.

"Better yet."

"See what you mean. Okay, sure. I'm game if you're game."

The Ace's presence had been duly noted, by this time. Damon was casting dark glances and La Carpa was giving him a high sign. A couple of the new faces were regarding him with open curiosity.

Bolan ignored the dark glances, returned the high sign, and instructed Leo, "Stay at my left hand, pal."

He strode directly to the master's desk, and placed the books down there. All eyes were now upon him, and the chatter had quickly died away. In a voice which carried clearly throughout that busy room, he snarled at Leo, "Give me that rotten fucking chair!"

Leo picked up on it immediately. He gave the master's chair a vicious kick and sent it rolling into Bolan's outstretched hand.

The Black Ace from the headshed thereupon hoisted that "rotten fucking chair" high overhead and brought it crashing to the desktop. It splintered and pieces of it bounced onto the conference table. All those guys out there were frozen in dumbfounded reaction to the outlandish ferocity of that act. So Bolan did it again, then flung the wreckage at the table. The disintegrating chair slid along the entire length of that glossy surface, the bulk of it falling at the stunned Mario Cuba's feet.

Not a goddamn murmur came back.

Bolan picked up the books and slammed them viciously onto the desk, the report of that impact slicing the heavy atmosphere in there like a rifle crack.

"Forty million bucks!" he yelled. "Did you know that? Forty *million!* It's the rottenest piece of shit I ever came across in all my years on this job! So I am vacating the chair of that thieving son-of-a-bitch! If anybody here don't like it . . . meaning if they love being robbed by their own father . . . then now's the time to say their say! Because I, by God, in the name of *all* the fathers, am declaring that the chair *never* existed! So say your say!"

He was glaring malevolently at Mario Cuba. The big guy dropped stunned eyes and said nothing.

"Not a murmur.

"Tony?"

Silence reigned.

"*Any* of you boys?"

No, not one of them.

"Today is Friday! On Monday, in New York, we carve up forty million bucks! Most of that, I'd say, belongs right here! But that will be for *you* to say! Because this kingdom does not exist! This *family*, I guess, *died* with the *first* father, Arnie the Farmer! Everything that came since Arnie is now declared null and void, it *never* existed! I write it off, here and now!"

He slammed the books down again.

Robert Damon flinched, the first real movement since the chair first came crashing down.

"Anybody with a say will be in New York on Monday morning at eight o'clock sharp! *Until* that time, *this* goddam family does not exist!"

"Now wait a minute, Frankie," Damon said weakly.

"*Some*body has been waiting too many minutes already," Frankie the Ace replied, appearing to cool off a bit, if the amplitude of the voice was any measure. He flicked an imaginary speck from his lapel, and said, "I can't believe you guys sat and let this happen. Where's your pride? Where the hell is your *faith* in the organization? You don't have to hold still for this kind of crap. That's what the organization is for . . . to establish reason and justice for all its members. It's us against the world, boys. If we lose ourselves, then what the hell have we got?"

Robert Damon's voice was still a bit shaky as he inquired, "What's that about Monday morning again?"

"Eight o'clock sharp," Bolan replied calmly. "Be there if you want representation. You too, Tony. You two are the logical heirs. But you first have to prove a claim. You have to show that a family exists."

"I, uh, guess I don't really understand what . . ."

"Then you better talk to Larry Haggle. It's about time you found out what's going on inside your own turf. That is, if you figure you *got* any turf."

The guy took no apparent offense whatever at that. He merely locked baffled eyes with La Carpa and said nothing.

"If you want my counsel, I'll give it," Bolan went on. "The two of you sit down and put the heads together. Make one head out of two. Draw up a charter. Lay out the new empire. Make it fair and equal. Then bring it to the headshed on Monday morning. Nobody up there wants to see you screwed. None of you. But they *do* want to see that you've got it together, that there's something here worth saving. And they're *not* going to throw no forty million bucks at a bunch of street punks. Get that understood. You return to grace. Get it together. Bring it to New York. You'll get justice. First, of course, you've got to get past Mack Bolan."

He tucked the books under his arm, threw an eye at Leo Turrin, and walked the hell out of there.

As they hit the hallway, Leo muttered, "Jesus Christ almighty! I never saw such a performance! They might make you boss of bosses!"

Not much chance of that, though.

By Monday, with a bit of luck, *all* the bosses would be gone . . . all the chairs vacated . . . at least for a little while.

The kingdoms of evil were nearing their rotten end. And not even a bona fide Frankie the Ace could save them from that.

CHAPTER 14

ALIVE AND LIVING

"Let me tell you," Leo muttered, "you had my flesh crawling awhile ago with that stuff about the Baldaserras. But I see, then, why you did it. Two stiffs to account for. But tell me . . . who really cut Tommy, do you think?"

Bolan had paused in the lobby to light a cigarette. He replied, very quietly over the flame, "Carmen Reddi did it."

Leo was scandalized by that. "Aw, *no!* The *house* boss?"

"The same," Bolan said. "It's a damned sick family, isn't it?"

"God, I guess it is!"

"Let's get the hell out of here," Bolan suggested, smiling faintly.

"I'm with you, pal. You got some wheels?"

"No. But I guess we'll find some."

Right on cue, then, Jimmy Jenner came loping up from the rear hall to breathlessly announce, "Your chopper's here, Frankie."

Bolan looked past his cigarette to check his watch, and took it like a trooper. "Great. Right on time."

This Jimmy Jenner was one of those guys who never grow old. He'd been around for years and years. Leo remembered him from the old days. Not exactly retarded or anything like that, but just forever laid back and taking it one day at a time. And the guy never grew old. He'd been a "kid" for as long as Leo could remember seeing him around.

And God was he impressed with this Frankie the Ace.

"Is it okay with you, Frankie, if I come off watch now? I just been standing around out there talking to my relief."

Bolan grinned and told that guy. "If we had forty like you, Jimmy, we could take the world."

The "kid" swelled noticeably under that praise. "I do my best. You say stay, I stay till you say different. And, Frankie, I just want to say if you'll pardon me, it's a pleasure to know you. I hope we see you again soon."

Bolan was giving with the solemn gaze. He laid it straight on the guy and asked him. "Will you take a word of quiet advice?"

"Yes, sir, whatever you say."

"Beat it."

"Huh?"

"Those men in there are going crazy. Take whoever you think you can trust to be quiet about it, and get the hell out of here. I don't mean tomorrow and I don't mean tonight, I mean right now. Go south. Go *far* south. And don't look back, don't ever look back."

"God, Frankie, what—"

"Do you get any meaning?"

"Yes, sir, I guess I get your meaning. And thanks. Thanks all to hell. I'll do like you say."

"Quietly."

The guy rolled his eyes and replied, "Bet your ass, quietly."

Bolan and Turrin went on outside, leaving Jimmy Jenner to ponder the troubling vicissitudes of a crumbling lifestyle.

As soon as they had cleared the door, Turrin growled, "*What* chopper?"

"Beats me," Bolan replied nonchalantly. "Let's go see."

"You beat all I ever . . . right on time, eh? And that boy Jenner—why'd you do that?"

The iron man shrugged and replied, "Why not? He's just a cipher in the games these people play. I get no pleassure from their blood. And the world doesn't need it. I'm going to level this joint, Leo. Let all that want to leave, leave. Those that stay will stay forever."

The undercover fed shivered as he digested that grim pronouncement. "I thought maybe you were getting soft spots," he muttered. "But the thought should perish."

Bolan squeezed the arm affectionately and told his old pal, "Maybe there is a soft spot here and there. Some of these kids . . . well . . ."

"Well, what?"

"I don't know, maybe I could buy the *Cosa Nostra* routine if it was pointed in the right direction. There's something very admirable about —it's like the military, when you take the military seriously. I never could believe in every man for himself. That's the larger danger of democracy. If people lose the spirit, then democracy deteriorates damn quick into anarchy. Anarchy is disorder, and disorder is anti-life. So . . ."

Turrin could not believe that they were having this conversation. The helipad was out near the docks, still fifty or so yards away. They had just left a pack of wild beasts to the rear, also an overgrown stray cub, who right now could be dashing about telling everybody within earshot that "Frankie says" everyone should bail out—strolling nonchalantly toward a helicopter which, for all anyone knew, could be carrying a genuine Ace of Spades or whatever—and the guy was talking casually about democracy, and disorder, and anti-life.

Leo growled, "What do you mean by anti-life?"

The big man shrugged and replied, "Even the merest speck of life depends on tight organization to survive. If it starts getting disorganized, then the plunge is quick and straight into entropy, the reversal of life. That, pal, I call anti-life."

Leo smiled weakly and said, "Okay." He always felt like such an idiot around this guy.

One day, maybe, if they both should live so long, he might actually figure out what made the guy tick. For now, Leo just felt fortunate as hell that the guy was ticking along right beside him.

The chopper was a commercial type of moderate size, capable of hauling three or four passengers probably. The engine coughed to life when they were about twenty paces out, sending the two boys on the dock watch retreating from the windstorm.

Bolan stepped aboard first, then gave Leo a hand and hauled him in without so much as a glance into the interior of that craft.

The guy at the controls looked vaguely familiar—a mob pilot, no doubt about that. Thank God for charmed lives, or whatever it was that kept the incredible Bolan alive and well, no one else was aboard.

But then it became immediately obvious that this *was* Bolan's chopper. The pilot leaned over to slap the big guy on the shoulder and muss his hair, then they were lifting away and sliding along the shoreline in a quick git.

The noise level in there made conversation damn near impossible, so Leo didn't even try for an understanding. He settled back into his seat, and took the first easy breath of that harrowing morning.

Bolan had his head right beside the pilot's. Apparently those two were having no problems with interpersonal communications. Bolan was grinning, and the pilot was waving a hand

145

around and shouting something, which got lost two inches from his mouth.

Some kind of guy, yeah, that Bolan. Hell, he could charm a charging rhino and turn its charge into a waltz with a flash of the eyes. It was no wonder, not in Leo Turrin's mind, that the mob was buckling and falling apart everywhere this guy happened to cast his attention. The goddam guy could just walk in and take over whatever he decided to take over. He could kill them with a smile, and win their rotten little hearts with a word and a swagger.

And yet there was no swagger to the real Mack Bolan. Leo had never met a finer man, a nicer guy, a more perfect human being. He was what every man, in his own secret heart, imagined that he himself could really be. Bolan was the *man*.

And sometimes Leo felt a little queer when he realized how he himself felt about that guy. So far as he knew, Leo had never *loved* another man. Not *love*, not even his own father. But, by God, he loved Mack Bolan. Let the world think of that what they would. Not that he wanted to lie down between the sheets with the guy, nothing like that for Christ's sake. But the love was there, and Leo was not all that sure that he would *not* lie down with the guy . . . if Mack Bolan turned out to be a little bit queer.

But that was crazy. There was nothing like that. Thank God. Leo had enough troubles already. And he knew that he was just feeling giddy, silly with the relief of being able to just walk out of that joint with his head still on his shoulders.

He wondered if anyone would ever really know . . . he meant, really *know*, just how close they'd both been to death and dismemberment all the time they were in that joint. *Leo* knew . . . and he figured that Bolan knew, too.

But no one else could know.

Bolan made it look so damned easy. Leo *knew* that it was not that easy. Those guys back there were nobody's damn fools. They were the most vicious, the most cunning, and the most by God *dangerous* sons-of-bitches between Atlantic City and Miami.

But that goddamn Bolan had done it to them again, hadn't he?

Right now, back there in that joint, they were all probably starting to tear each other apart. And here sat Bolan, relaxed and grinning and having a nice visit with another old pal.

Leo recognized that pilot, now. The name was Grimaldi. He'd been a genuine member of the clan, once. But the redoubtable Sarge had wooed and won the guy somewhere between Vegas and San Juan—and, like so many others, the world had never again been the same for Jack Grimaldi.

Okay, dammit, call it love.

Nothing wrong with that.

Hell. Bolan had his finger right on it. It was reversed entropy. It was *life*. And *living* it *large*. It was two human beings *knowing* that the world was a better place simply because *they* were *together*.

Not a damned thing in the world wrong with that, just because it happens between a couple of guys.

But those men back there . . . those other men . . .

Yeah. The Sarge had put the finger right on it. Those men back there were *anti*-life.

CHAPTER 15

THE SPECIALISTS

The promontory had become a bit crowded. Three big "tour buses" had joined the warwagon there, and "Brognola's cavalry"—a highly professional force of roughly three dozen federal marshals—were deployed about in casual groups of "sightseers," as a very effective screen to block the area off from any civilians who might happen by.

Brognola himself stepped forward to greet the men at the helicopter. Leo Turrin was the first man out. The chief fed grabbed the little guy in a crunching bear hug and told him, "Good work, Sticker, damned good work!"

Bolan was right behind. The chief went for him, too, quickly wrapping him in an emotional embrace, whereupon the three of them joined in a spontaneous, but clumsy, little dance.

An emotional bunch, this, yes. It could be

that way, for those who lived at the heartbeat—
as Mack would say—unless fear and suspicion
and ambition overcame.

April leapt from the warwagon and made a
determined bid to find her place amidst all
that masculiinty. Bolan saw her coming, and
reached out with a strong arm to include her
in.

She caught a glimpse of some marshals off
to the side of that reunion, grinning at each
other and joining vicariously in the celebra-
tion. Then she was totally off her feet and
swept into the all-encompassing embrace of
her man.

And, yes God, it was good.

Jack Grimaldi came out of the chopper with
Santelli's books under his arm. Brognola whirled
to receive that treasure, whooping happily
something about "the gold-dust bust."

April had never seen the chief with his hair
so totally down.

Bolan set her down onto her feet, whispering
to her, "Later," and turning back to confer
with Brognola.

"Have you been reading me, Hal?"

"All the way, you bet. And we have a make
on your *Tangier Victory*. She got underway at
dawn, now running south toward Cape Henry.
We got a fax copy of the manifest from Cus-
toms. Supposedly she's hauling nothing but machine parts to Amsterdam. But we have a passenger list, too. She's carrying a Zurich money-

man and two brokers, who have been buying up oil storage leases in Europe for the past year. CIA already had tabs on those guys. Eighteen more passengers are all males, all foreign nationals, and all starting to look very suspicious in the initial checkout. I'd call it an armed guard. So, I think it's pay dirt for sure."

"Is it legal to haul gold and silver?"

"Not the way they're doing it, no."

"So all you have to do now is get authority to board and search," Bolan observed casually.

"Uh, well, there's a hitch."

Bolan growled, "It figures."

"Yeah. That ship is operating under Algerian registry. There is a, quote, sensitive status, unquote, seal over at State Department covering anything Algerian, which simply translates to *hands off.*"

"Can't that seal be broken?"

"Sure. As soon as we resolve a couple of small diplomatic crises with Algeria regarding certain covert African activities."

Bolan cast a dark glance at April as he commented, "You're telling me we're losing it again to diplomacy."

"Don't get your tail kinked. We're working the problem. It may take a couple of days, but—"

"No."

"We can make the bust anywhere. We can make it in Amsterdam."

"No way. The farther away it gets, the more uncertain it all becomes. That shipment is not leaving American waters."

Brognola was becoming greatly uncomfortable. "You expect us to declare war on Algeria, dammit?"

"Not you, no," Bolan replied quietly.

"Aw, look, Striker . . ."

"Just turn your back, Hal."

"Dammit, no! There's no need. We can keep the damned ship under surveillance clear across the pond if need be. We'll have the full cooperation of—"

"Huh-uh, not good enough."

"You can't attack a damned!—you'll have the Coast Guard and everyone else all over your ass, and I can't do a—tomorrow's *Saturday*, Striker! *One more day* and we're home free! Let's not blow it now, not for a . . ."

"For what?" Bolan prodded coolly. "For a clear and present victory? For the knockout punch? I'm not playing diplomatic games with these people, Hal. They used an Algerian registry for no other reason than security and evasion. You know that as well as I do. If Algeria wants to run her flag into our troubled waters, then so be it. She can take her lumps with the rest of them. But it's just a flag, and everyone at State knows that. Who owns the vessel?"

Brognola dropped his eyes and replied, "A consortium operating out of Rotterdam."

"A consortium of what?"

"Uh, financial wheeler-dealers, I guess."

"Free market wheeler-dealers."

"I guess."

"Okay. If it makes you more comfortable, turn your back. But I'm taking them." He clasped April's hand and threw an eye on Grimaldi. "You game, pal?"

The pilot grinned, and raised his shoulders in an exaggerated shrug. "Why not?"

Brognola ground his teeth together and growled, "Okay, I'll backboard it all I can. Once you hit, then I guess the vessel is in distress and—okay, I'll see if I can jerk some tails at Coast Guard. But, dammit, don't do anything nutty!"

The chief fed grabbed Leo Turrin and dragged him toward the official mobile command post.

Bolan smiled faintly and muttered, "Poor Hal." Then he led the way to his own combat center, pulling Grimaldi and April along in a close clutch to either side.

"You take care of the armaments," he instructed the pilot as they boarded the warwagon. "Take a couple of light subs and plenty of ammo. And, uh, the bazooka . . . and some AP rounds."

"I'd settle for a couple of aerial bombs," Grimaldi said jokingly.

Bolan smiled. "Okay. I'll build a couple right quick."

"You serious?"

"Sure, I'm serious. Would, uh, you load the

other stuff, Jack? I want a minute with April."

The pilot winked and went on back to the weapons lab.

Bolan took off his coat, reached inside the shoulder, and carefully removed a tiny micro-pickup. It was about the size of a quarter, and had a six-inch, filament-like wire extending from it. "How'd it work?" he asked the girl.

April suddenly felt strangely ill at ease, almost embarrassed. "Beautifully," she reported, in a barely audible voice. "Never lost touch for a moment. Where'd you put the micro-relay?"

He smiled and said, "I ran it up their flag-pole."

That hit her as very funny, dispelling the edgy feeling. "Seriously?" she squealed, clapping her hands together delightedly.

"Sure." He flashed her a wide grin. "Just clipped it to the halyard and ran it up the pole. Long may it wave."

"You really *are* something else, you know," she said, lapsing again into the jitters—adding, as a whisper, "Captain Thunder."

He caught that whisper. "I could have turned it off, you know. Or *you* could have."

She replied, "No, I . . . not that you were . . . look, I want to get this out front with us. I've thought about it and . . . well, dammit, Striker, I wouldn't have you any other way. I mean, it's . . . it's warm and it's . . . right."

"Toby is very special," he softly explained.

"I know. And you are very special. All of you

154

crazy people are very special. I just . . . I guess I feel sort of . . . left out. Know what I mean?"

Bolan replied, those great eyes brooding down on her, "April, you are what makes it special. Don't ever start feeling that way. I don't want you down there in hell, not ever again. You've seen the doorway and that's enough. April, love, there has to be something waiting in heaven, or hell simply isn't worth it."

She began crying, hating herself for it, despising the damned feminine tears and trying to choke them back. Worst of all, he was letting her have the moment—holding her in very tight and gently massaging her back.

She quickly pushed clear of that, reasserting control. "Do you have to be so damned beautiful?" she asked, laughing quietly and striving for lightness. "All this heaven and hell stuff . . . it was very beautiful what you said to Toby. And I guess I just felt like a damned eavesdropper. You *should* have turned it off, you know. I wouldn't want anyone listening in on *us.*"

"How do you know they're not?" he whispered, raising his eyebrows in mock alarm and glancing furtively about.

"Mack, I love you!" she cried, and the damned waterworks came back full force.

"If you're going to wet me down," he said gruffly, "you could at least take me to the shower."

"Is that an invitation?" she whispered through the tears.

Grimaldi went noisily past at that moment with a load of weaponry. "I'll, uh, be about five minutes," he informed them, very pointedly.

Bolan was going into a stripdown, seemingly all business again. "I'll need the blacksuit," he told her.

She went blindly to the wardrobe and found the combat outfit. But when she turned about, her man was nowhere in view. The clothing he had been wearing was folded neatly across a console.

Then she heard the water start, in the shower.

Grimaldi was halfway to the chopper.

She closed the door and threw the interlocks, then left a trail of her own clothing from console to shower stall.

"Knock knock," she said breathlessly.

A strong arm reached past the curtain and hauled her in.

"Lord, but you're beautiful!" she sighed.

Indeed, indeed. To *hell* with *hell!*

If *this* was heaven, April had certainly found her niche. And, yes, she felt very special.

CHAPTER 16

INCIDENT AT SEA

They overtook the vessel at one of the wider points at this end of the nearly 200-mile long bay—roughly twenty miles across from shore to shore, if you discounted a couple of small islands and a jagged peninsula extending from the eastern side.

She was a tired old freighter of WW2 vintage, drafting perhaps five thousand tons under full load, though now riding high and apparently running under very light load.

Grimaldi went in close for target verification, crabbing about at mast level to run along the keel line in a fore-to-aft pass at about fifty yards out.

A guy in the wheelhouse stepped to a side window to peer at them through binoculars as they slid by.

"That's her," Grimaldi shouted.

"You figure about ten knots?"

"More or less, yeah. What's the plan of attack?"

"Give me a hover as close as you can get to that wheelhouse."

"Are we shooting or spitting?"

"Let's try first for spit," Bolan yelled back, grinning. He snared the portable electronic bullhorn and added, "Any time you're ready."

The amazing flyman was always ready. No sooner said than done, Bolan found himself in an eye to eye confrontation with a scowling mariner in a gold-braided hat. He told that guy, via the bullhorn, "I'll give you two minutes to abandon ship. Shut down the engines, drop the hook, and bail out. Two minutes. Then I blow this tub out of the water."

The guy just gawked at him, but Bolan knew that the message had been received and understood. Two wild-eyed guys in civilian dress ran out onto the bridge deck to assist in the gawking. Another man stepped through a hatch on the main deck, waving a revolver and shouting something to others still inside and out of sight.

"I want no innocent blood," Bolan informed one and all. He tossed a marksman's medal through the open window of the wheelhouse. A guy in there reacted as though it were a grenade, diving for cover behind the bulkhead. "I just want your cargo. But you guys have to call the play. Those that stay will have to pay. Two minutes from now. *Two* minutes."

He did not have to say a word to Grimaldi. The hot combat pilot immediately cocked the rotor, and sent the little chopper swinging into a quick withdrawal to a safe holding range.

"Think they'll take it?" Grimaldi shouted above the rotor noise.

Bolan shrugged his shoulders and began readying the weaponry. "One way or another," he growled.

His only concern was for the seamen. Those guys had no stake in any of this—though, certainly, the skipper and, maybe, all the ship's officers must have been wise. Bona fide "passengers" do not cavort about the decks of their vessel brandishing weapons.

He would sincerely prefer that the non-combatants get the hell out of the way. But their continued presence there, after fair warning, would not prolong the life of that ill-fated freighter.

Grimaldi crowed, "There they go! A raft just hit the water!"

Someone, yes, was taking the warning seriously.

Not one raft, but two were now in the water beside the ship, trailing along at the end of towlines. And several men were over the side already.

So okay.

The option was there and some were taking it.

There could be no overriding concern for the others.

"A minute thirty!" the pilot reported.

Bolan loaded the bazooka and positioned it in the open doorway. From a satchel at his feet he removed a molded ball of plastic explosive, and carefully inserted an impact detonator.

Grimaldi rolled the eyes and yelled, "You were serious!"

"Always," Bolan replied. "And we'd better stay serious about this stuff. It's heavy goods. We don't want to be too close to the hit."

"Roger, understood. Just tell me when."

Bolan looked at his watch and made a hand signal. "Once across the bow for starters. Strafing run."

Sure . . . no sooner said than done.

The little bird kicked itself into a side-slipping plunge and executed a wide turn to starboard, shooting an angle which cut an intercepting path directly across the bow and a hundred feet above the deck of the *Tangier Victory.*

Grimaldi had jury-rigged a tripod mount on his side, on which was positioned a light submachine gun. Bolan wedged a foot into a deck cleat, and knelt in the doorway with a hand-held chatterpiece.

They side-slipped across the path of the moving vessel, and raked the decks with a withering fire, going not for blood but for pure psychological effect. And they got plenty of that. Grimaldi ended the side-swing with an abrupt vertical rise and a hover at two hundred feet,

160

the vessel passing almost directly beneath them. Someone had cut the towlines to the two rafts, and people were slipping overboard from both sides of the ship.

But they got a bit more than psychological effect, as well. They got return fire, from more than a dozen points below. A couple of guys on the bridge were using rifles, and one on the fantail cut loose with a burst from an auto, which sliced across the after section of the 'copter.

Grimaldi kicked her again and went into a windmilling climb across the port quarter, swinging far out and going into a wide circular path, once again angling for an intercept.

Guys were scrambling all over those decks down there, now, guys with weapons looking for cover and awaiting a kill.

Bolan had offered the crew all the consideration he could afford. He could see numerous bodies in the water, bobbing about in a long and irregular path in the vessel's wake. As for the others . . .

"Stay and pay, boys," he muttered to himself; then, to Grimaldi, "Bomb run!"

"Bomb run, aye," the pilot yelled back, and kicked the little ship into a head-on confrontation at full throttle.

They zoomed in at about two hundred feet, Bolan kneeling in the open doorway with his homemade aerial bomb. He flipped it out as they broke the bow, yelling, "*Away!*"

161

Grimaldi's quick evasive maneuver very nearly flung Bolan through the doorway; it was as though some giant hand had reached down from the heavens to snatch up the little craft and hurl it away. Good thing, too. It was *damned* heavy goods. Impact was just forward the superstructure, main deck. The blow was primarily aft, the blast throwing its major effect toward the superstructure and bathing the entire forward bulkhead in a huge mushroom of fire.

The chopper was five hundred feet off the deck, and maybe a hundred yards to starboard before the full effect could be evaluated.

The window glass of the wheelhouse was shattered and gone, paint blistered and blackened. The seaman at the wheel had obviously given it up; the ship was off her course, now, still steaming but beginning to wander to starboard in a diagonal line across the shipping channel.

Secondary fires were erupting around the cargo hatch forward, and there was much human excitement down there.

They went in again, Bolan hoping for a hundred-to-one knockout punch down the stack with the second and last bomb, but it was not to be. Those gunners down there were throwing up a hell of an effective fire now. The chopper was taking hits everywhere, slugs punching through the thin skin like hail through tissue paper. Grimaldi had to opt for caution as a better alternative; the homemade bomb missed the superstructure entirely, dropping onto the after cargo deck and raising another firestorm back there.

"It's getting rough!" the pilot yelled, as once again they swung up to a safe hover. "What d'ya think?"

"I need to be sure!" Bolan yelled back. "I want the wheelhouse!"

"Okay, swell. How do you figure to get it?"

"Bazooka range!"

"Yeah, I was afraid you'd say that! You'll need a stable platform! And you can't fire that thing off inside here! The backburn could play hell with this bird!"

"Get me a platform, then! I need a trajectory straight into the wheelhouse!"

"That could be tougher than you think! It looks like nobody's steering that vessel, now! She's yawing the channel!"

Bolan yelled, "Get out in front and hang there! Hold her at fifty feet off the deck! As stable as possible! I want her to slide right under us!"

"At fifty feet she'll slide right through us! The bridge is higher than that!"

"I want a horizontal sightline into that bridge! You can haul away the moment I release my bird!"

"The return fire will be murderous at that range! Are you sure you want this?"

"I want it, yeah. But I can't tell *you* to do it!"

163

"Hell, I want it if you want it! I'll do it! Okay, here's the only way I can do it! Can you hear me?"

"Go ahead, I hear!"

"I'll have to take her bow-on, tail-high just a bit! That will make the angle for my gun so I can give you some cover! But that means you've got to fire across our own bow! You get my meaning! You've got to be *outside*! So the blowback doesn't rupture our nest And you're going to be a hanging duck! Do you get my meaning?"

Bolan got his meaning, sure. He'd have to brace himself against the landing skid, get that big bazooka onto the shoulder, and wait for a line-up. Meanwhile those people below were going to have a stationary target to plunk at.

"Let's go do it!" he shouted.

So they went and did it. The vessel was still yawing hard to starboard, and lining into a dead run toward the distant west shore. Grimaldi circled out to an intercepting point, while Bolan positioned himself in the doorway and studied the man-angle between doorway and skid.

As it so often turns out, the contemplation of the act was the hardest part. Grimaldi successfully anticipated the intercept course of the rapidly yawing vessel and took station at fifty feet above that path. Bolan slipped outside and settled himself onto the skid, straddling it and steadying himself against the fuselage. Then he dragged the bazooka outside and hoisted it to the right shoulder.

Several men with rifles ran into the open on the ship's bow and took up firing positions. The vessel was approaching at a speed of roughly ten knots. The riflemen below opened fire. Grimaldi responded with his sub, lacing it into them with telling effect from about a hundred yards out, scattering them and disrupting the defensive set.

The worst part, for Bolan, was the waiting.

The men on deck were scattering to cover and continuing the duel with Grimaldi, but only half-heartedly.

Bolan sat on his skid and waited, eye at the scope, ticking off the slowly dwindling range, waiting it in, loathe to waste a round and have to scramble around for a reload from this precarious perch.

He could see the men on deck clearly now, could read their faces . . . knew that they were not American Mafia . . . wondered about the connection with foreign interests . . . thought back over the developments of this fantastically telescoped morning on the day of the vulture . . . wondered about the man with the gold braid, who was now staggering across the wheelhouse toward that unmanned ship's wheel . . . wondered if the guy . . .

And then he knew he could not do it.

He could not send a killing firestorm into that housing. That poor guy, very probably, was not the enemy, but just a seaman doing his job, following company orders . . . master of a vessel in deep trouble and getting deeper with each passing moment. This was not cops and robbers . . . and it was not even war . . . not in Mack Bolan's sense of the word.

It was, hell, an incident at sea . . . and it was just too damned impossible to separate the innocent from the guilty.

Bolan lowered the sights and squeezed into the fire. The rocket whooshed out of there and made a trail of flame to the impact point on the bow of the vessel, expanding then into a shattering fireball, which enwrapped men, rifles, and all into its consuming grasp.

Then he reloaded and did it again, sending this one into another defiant pocket at the forward mast.

He could see the face of the man at the wheel, now, very clearly. The guy was ringing something up on the engine telegraph . . . and Bolan could tell by the position of the levers that it was ALL ENGINES STOP.

He heaved the bazooka inside, and pulled himself back aboard. The 'copter immediately swung away from the collision course with the ship's bridge, the pilot yelling, "Jesus! What happened?"

"Enough already," Bolan yelled back. He donned the headset and asked Brognola, "Where the hell is the Coast Guard?"

"They're on the way, Striker," was the quick reply. "Get the hell out of there!"

"Get the hell out of here, Jack," Bolan said tiredly to his pilot. "Forty million American bucks are at all engines stop . . . and ready for salvage."

CHAPTER 17

TRICK OF TIME

Incredibly, it seemed, the forward progress of Friday, Day of the Feast, had reached no farther than eleven o'clock A.M. Bolan felt as though the day had already consumed a full week of 24-hour days. As for the past week, itself . . . well, yeah . . . infinite lives. And he wondered if infinity itself was no more than a trick of time, a telescoping of large moments against some vast backdrop called eternity.

The distressed freighter, *Tangier Victory*, was foundering in the shipping channel of Chesapeake Bay, the Coast Guard aboard and fire boats alongside. The early report from the authorities bore no mention of combat at sea, dead and wounded, or forty million dollars in gold and silver; it merely stated that an explosion and fires had disabled the vessel, and that all crew members were alive and safe.

The direct report from Brognola, though, was much more reassuring. The mob money had been quickly located and was being transferred to a cutter. There would be some legal hassles over that illicit fortune, no doubt, but for damn sure it was going nowhere quickly—and its very presence was going to be greatly embarrassing to a number of American businessmen, legitimate and otherwise.

All of which satisfied Mack Bolan's frame of reference to the matter, the whole point being that the mob had suffered another staggering loss in its financial department. Coupled with the other losses of this week, not to mention all that had disappeared earlier, it seemed unlikely that the organization could survive this one. Maybe service *was* power, as Larry Haggle had so convincingly claimed, but it took a lot of dimes and dollars to manage the clout machines and political gamesmanship that corrupted power and enthroned it. And, of course, genuine service with a fair return on investment was the American way; there was no need to fear honorable men with enterprising ideas. There was also no place in the Mafia mentality for *fair* return or honorable enterprise.

So, yes, Friday's battle could certainly be regarded as a death blow. Bolan could take heart if this had been the full extent of the day's results.

But, then, there was that other matter . . .

The banquet table had been prepared, yet only a few had feasted. Mack Bolan had been a phantom guest at that table, and had left with hardly a taste. That was no way for a guest of honor to quit the feast.

So here he was, back once more . . . contemplating the fate of that old joint beside the bay, this time by the full light of day.

April Rose was manning the warwagon, holding at a position within range of the cruiser's rocketry and visual surveillance systems, on a high overlook to the south.

Grimaldi was standing by in the shot-up chopper, ready to lend a hand should a hand from the sky be needed.

Bolan had radio communications with both, via a small two-way rig in the shoulder pocket of the blacksuit. He was also loaded for heavy combat. Besides the usual personal weapons, he now carried in a shoulder sling an M-16/203 combination, and wore a flak vest with pockets to hold a full assortment of 40mm rounds for the 203 (the mated designation for the M-79). Also on the bod and dangling in quick-release attachments were four hand-throw grenades and two smoke canisters. In a special backpack were carefully nestled a number of plastic strips already impregnated with timer-detonators.

If all that stuff were to go off prematurely, on the bod, the two hundred pounds or so representing the physical existence of one Mack Bolan would violently disperse itself in microscopic bits to the far recesses of the universe . . . and, yeah, that could be a trick of time, too.

The trick right now, of course, was to send some other bits and pieces to the universe . . . to destroy a symbol of most everything that had ever been wrong with America . . . to put a final seal on the victory at Baltimore.

He spoke into his shoulder, saying, "Do you see me?"

April's tense tones bounced right back at him: "Affirm, have you in sight, beautiful."

"Let's have a one-two. Send number one to the attic window, number two into the wall at three-six-zero from my present position."

"The fire is ready," she replied a moment later.

"Then send it," he growled.

It came instantly, a fire-tailed serpent sizzling directly overhead in a doomsday course to the attic window of Arnie Farmer's old joint beside the bay, another hotting along close behind and dipping to plow itself with shattering force into the stone wall. Twin firestorms flung themselves into hot and instant destruction, one whole section of roof blowing away and scattering its parts onto the grounds, while the fire devoured all that remained within its area of influence; the other sending shattered shards of razor-sharp stone in a driving horizontal rain onto those grounds, and leaving a gaping void inhabited only by smoke and flame where once had proudly stood the symbol of domain.

Bolan was up and running with the first overhead sizzle, plunging from fifty yards out toward the hole which he knew would materialize in that forward defense. A pretty voice from his shoulder urged, "Be careful!" as he hit the smoke and whirled on through to the goodies inside.

But she would not really desire that he take time for "careful" on these hellgrounds if she really knew the score.

A stone-imbedded body lay motionless twenty feet inside the wall. He leapt over it and threw forty flaming millimeters of eager HE into a window of a garage apartment, following through with an immediate five-second burst of 5.56 fleshseekers into another.

People were scampering about and yelling all around him as he flipped out a smoke canister, and added that little confusion factor to the erupting pandemonium.

A wild-eyed guy with a double-barrel shotgun came charging around the back corner, and immediately pulled both triggers straight into the ground at his feet. The guy tumbled down screaming, shy a foot; Bolan sent him a zip across the chest to finish neatly what the poor guy had started sloppily for himself—then whirled to confront another movement through the smoke on his flank.

A guy whom he instantly recognized as a La Carpa lieutenant was running full tilt at the head of a pack of four, coming in from the front wall in ghastly appreciation of the event that obviously all had been awaiting.

Bolan was glad that he had not disappointed his hosts.

He dropped to one knee and thumbed in another HE round, letting it fly at the same instant that the lieutenant halted his headlong flight with the brakes to the floor, mouth agape and arms flailing as he tried to signal those behind him that dreadful fulfillment lay dead ahead. Too late, though, came the horrified realization. Those guys were in collision and falling all over one another when the HE joined their little gathering. Bolan did not pause for an evaluation, but whirled again and lobbed a short-fused grenade through a downstairs window as he jogged on into hell.

The front door disintegrated under the pummeling assault of another forty flaming millimeters, and Bolan ran through without pause.

If pandemonium was the word for outside, then frantic panic was the tag for that scene in there.

Robert Damon lay just inside the shattered doorway with one side of his face missing, the body still twitching in the death throes. Another shattered man lay beneath him. A fire was raging in the old parlor, and a flaming body had toppled out of there into the foyer as Bolan entered. La Carpa and two of his boys were falling back from that unsettling scene in a pell-mell retreat toward the rear hall.

One of those guys danced around and popped a couple of quick shots from a revolver, neither of them coming anywhere near Bolan. He sent a quick floral wreath from the M-16, which wrapped itself in a figure-eight onto all three, and they ended their retreat in a bloody slide to nowhere.

Some unseen gunner with a chopper cut loose from the head of the stairs, chewing up a wall down below and raising hell with one of the rickety old couches, firing at God knew what—like, maybe, throwing a shoe at a phantom on the bedroom wall.

Bolan leaned into the stairwell and tossed a grenade up there, then went on into the study.

Mario Cuba lay in there with a long knife protruding from his chest; he'd been dead awhile. Billy Garante and one of La Carpa's crew bosses lay nearby, dead from gunshot wounds—also awhile in their demise.

So, yes, the enemy apparently had engaged itself in at least some brief dissension within the ranks.

The sliding panel to Santelli's "vault" was open. Carmen Reddi stood nervously in the opening, peering at something inside.

He felt, rather than saw Bolan's presence, turning to face him with frozen countenance and slumping shoulders. The "head waiter" clothing was no longer immaculate, but was now disheveled and bloodstained. The guy had a big welt running the width of his forehead, and his lower lip was puffed.

Mario, maybe.

But brute strength, as usual, apparently had been no match for ruthless wile.

This one, though, had no wiles left. The frozen face melted into sheer terror as those zooming eyes locked onto the imposing figure of Mack Bolan at war.

Frankie the Ace in blacksuit tossed a marksman's medal to the floor at the house boss's feet.

Carmen said, "Uh . . . uh . . ." and it was his final song. The '16 zipped him from hip to opposite shoulder, flinging him on into the master's retreat, and sprawling him to his knees at the master's bed as though in bedtime prayer.

Larry Haggle came out of there damned quick, a set of books clutched to his chest, panting in terror. He leaned into the wall at the edge of the sliding panel, bulging eyes staring uncomprehendingly at the little medal, which lay in that doorway.

"Can I be of *service*, counselor?" inquired Frankie the Ace.

"Aw . . . aw . . . aw, hell, Frankie."

"Wrong. Not Frankie. Try again."

"We already heard, yeah. A body in Lauderdale . . ." Those hot eyes could not, would not, contemplate the sight of what had come for him. They flung themselves to the more comfortable sight of his own hands as he thrust the precious books forward with stiff arms. "Here are the books," he gasped.

"You already gave me the books."

"Second set. Copy. My own."

"You trying to cop a plea, counselor?"

"Call it what . . . okay, sure, whatever. These . . . *real* books. Not forty. Fifty . . . fifty million. Shipped fifty . . ."

"You cut yourself in."

"Sure. Wouldn't you?" The *consigliere* was beginning to sound like, at least, a shadow of his old self—the voice becoming more confident, the training and habits of years reasserting some semblance of dignity. "Be sensible. All this money. We could own the world. Whole fucking world."

"We?"

"Sure. Who's to know?"

"Santelli wouldn't know."

"Even alive, no. Fuckin' dummy. Couldn't manage a personal checking account. This is big time, Frankie—uh, whoever."

"You can say my name. It doesn't hurt. So Santelli wasn't the robber."

The guy laughed—a sobbing, hysterical, dying sound. "Tommy couldn't rob himself. Playing around with his *hole* in Florida. What a sap! Like you . . . uh, no, I mean like you said Frankie said . . . I mean . . ."

"Romance," Bolan suggested frostily.

"Exactly. Crazy. Hole in the ground for God's sake. For what? For romance. Pirates and all that. Secret passageways to nowhere. For what? For *dope?* Come on. Come on now, Tommy! You want *dope?* We got the world by the ass, man. One poor sucker in a thousand wants *dope*.

177

Every son-of-a-bitch in the whole crying world wants *gas*. Service is power. *Gas* is the *ultimate* power."

"Wrong," Bolan quietly told that guy.

"No. Not wrong. It's—"

"Romance."

"Huh?"

"The dream is the power. The faith. The spirit, counselor."

"Bullshit, no. Here. Look at this."

The guy was thrusting the books stiffly forward, offering the keys to a bitter kingdom.

But he was offering them to the wrong guy.

The M-16 flashed the only response possible, a full fresh magazine feeding the spray, which laced out of there to disintegrate those books and punch on through into the spirit of depravity beyond.

Bolan followed the dancing body into the master's chamber, and kept on spraying until that magazine was empty.

Then he dropped another medal and muttered, "Long live the king."

For sure. Time had played its final trick at this joint.

The king was finally dead.

EPILOGUE

The flaming old wreck lifted herself in a final convulsion, borne aloft in fiery pieces by the demolition charges in her historic cellars.

Bolan killed the optics monitor, and sent the warwagon into quiet withdrawal.

His lady crouched behind him, arms about his neck and that smooth face pressed warmly against the warstained hide of his own.

"I'm going to wire you for sound from now on," she told him in a warm little voice. "And for video, too, if I can figure a way to rig it. I just love the sight and sound of you. Even at war. But especially at your dirty rat's best."

"Am I a dirty rat?"

"Dirtiest I ever heard. I mean the soft penetrations. Never hath a man spake with so forked a tongue. Oh, by the way, I have some video-

179

tape which might interest you. Sticker identified the subject. He says it's the New York boss, Marco Minotti."

"Where'd you find Marco?"

"Right out here. But not for long. He turned tail and split damned quick when he saw all the fireworks. He came in a three-car convoy, big limousines, New York plates."

Bolan commented, "Maybe that explains the Baldaserra brothers."

"That was Leo's reading."

"Leo?"

"Sticker schmicker—go to hell, Striker piker. I'm onto your damned games."

Bolan pulled abruptly to the side of the road and dragged the lady into his arms.

"I have games you haven't dreamed of, kid."

"Prove it."

"You really want me to prove it?"

"I really do, yes. I want you to prove it."

By all means, he would do that. The way time had shrunk . . . it had been amazingly short day in hell. Twenty more minutes would take care of the rendezvous with the mobile feds and the final wrap-up for Friday.

Saturday, of course . . . Saturday would be another day, and probably a damned long one.

"Is this still Friday?" he asked his lady.

"Of course, it's still Friday. Why?"

"It's the day of the feast."

"Really? What's on the menu?"

God, this kid was really asking for it. And he would, by God and thank God, give her everything she had coming . . . for as long as heaven might last.

the EXECUTIONER by Don Pendleton

☐	40-027-9	Executioner's War Book		$1.50
☐	40-299-6	War Against the Mafia	#1	1.50
☐	40-300-3	Death Squad	#2	1.50
☐	40-301-1	Battle Mask	#3	1.50
☐	40-302-X	Miami Massacre	#4	1.50
☐	40-303-8	Continental Contract	#5	1.50
☐	40-304-6	Assault on Soho	#6	1.50
☐	40-305-4	Nightmare in New York	#7	1.50
☐	40-306-2	Chicago Wipeout	#8	1.50
☐	40-307-0	Vegas Vendetta	#9	1.50
☐	40-308-9	Caribbean Kill	#10	1.50
☐	40-309-7	California Hit	#11	1.50
☐	40-310-0	Boston Blitz	#12	1.50
☐	40-311-9	Washington I.O.U.	#13	1.50
☐	40-312-7	San Diego Siege	#14	1.50
☐	40-313-5	Panic in Philly	#15	1.50
☐	40-314-3	Sicilian Slaughter	#16	1.50
☐	40-237-6	Jersey Guns	#17	1.50
☐	40-315-1	Texas Storm	#18	1.50
☐	40-316-X	Detroit Deathwatch	#19	1.50
☐	40-238-4	New Orleans Knockout	#20	1.50
☐	40-317-8	Firebase Seattle	#21	1.50
☐	40-318-6	Hawaiian Hellground	#22	1.50
☐	40-319-4	St. Louis Showdown	#23	1.50
☐	40-239-2	Canadian Crisis	#24	1.50
☐	40-224-4	Colorado Kill-Zone	#25	1.50
☐	40-320-8	Acapulco Rampage	#26	1.50
☐	40-321-6	Dixie Convoy	#27	1.50
☐	40-225-2	Savage Fire	#28	1.50
☐	40-240-6	Command Strike	#29	1.50
☐	40-150-7	Cleveland Pipeline	#30	1.50
☐	40-166-3	Arizona Ambush	#31	1.50
☐	40-252-X	Tennessee Smash	#32	1.50
☐	40-333-X	Monday's Mob	#33	1.50
☐	40-334-8	Terrible Tuesday	#34	1.50